Critical Praise for *America*

"Dark and quirky, a revealing excursion to a place over which 'the gringos' to the north always loom."

—*New York Times Book Review*

"Harrowing and hilarious." —*Boston Globe*

"Beautifully written, atmospheric, and stylish in the manner of Chandler . . . a smart, exotic crime fiction offering."

—George Pelecanos, author of *The Turnaround*

"Near-broke, provincial, middle-aged Mario Alvarez seems a bit like an older, only slightly wiser, but oddly more likable Holden Caulfield . . . A serious novel made palatable by humor as dry as the Andean uplands in which it is set."

—*Kirkus Reviews*

"This is a thriller with a social conscience, a contemporary noir with lots of humor and flair. The streets of La Paz have never looked so alive. This is one of the best Latin American novels of the last fifteen years."

—Edmundo Paz Soldán, author of *Turing's Delirium*

"A winning tale . . . Recacoechea makes Alvarez's crime less a puzzle than an intriguing window onto a society on the fringes of globalization."

—*Publishers Weekly*

"Recacoechea's novel is set in La Paz, Bolivia but its black-humored lines . . . come straight from noirland."

—*Washington City Paper*

"*American Visa* is a stunning literary achievement. It is insightful and poignant, a book every thoughtful American should read, and once read, read again."

—William Heffernan, Edgar Award–winning author of *The Corsican*

"Recacoechea's tale of a down-on-his-luck everyman is certainly gritty, but it's enlivened with enough comedy to keep it from feeling hopeless."

—*Chicago Reader*

"De Recacoechea celebrates the hybrid in ethnicity and culture, and he does it without reverence or even respect, blending absurdity with harsh realism to tell a surprising story of roots and finding home."

—*Booklist*

"Quite possibly Bolivia's baddest-ass book . . . *American Visa* shows La Paz, despite its altitude, is no place for the light-headed, nor the easily swayed. It shows, too, that a place not our own need not be taken for granted."

—*SunPost* (Miami)

"Mario Alvarez is tremendous, an everyman desperate to escape Bolivia's despair who can't elude his own tricks of self-sabotage. At a time when the debate around U.S. immigration reduces many people around the world to caricatures, this singular and provocative portrait of the issue will connect with readers of all political stripes."

—Arthur Nersesian, author of *Suicide Casanova*

"Recacoechea's first novel to be translated into English is filled with exciting events, colorful characters, and slapstick humor. Its fast pace will keep readers turning the pages."

—*MultiCultural Review*

"That the below-the-belt blows of Recacoechea's punch-drunk classic are delivered only to prevent a downtrodden dreamer from making it to Miami bring the story that much closer to home."

—*Flavorpill* (Miami)

Andean Express

a novel by

Juan de Recacoechea

translated by Adrian Althoff

Akashic Books
New York

This is a work of fiction. All names, characters, places, and incidents are the product of the author's imagination. Any resemblance to real events or persons, living or dead, is entirely coincidental.

Published by Akashic Books

Originally published in Spanish under the title *Altiplano Express* in 2000
by Alfaguara
Map by Aaron Petrovich

ISBN-13: 978-1-933354-72-9
Library of Congress Control Number: 2008937352

First printing

Akashic Books
PO Box 1456
New York, NY 10009
info@akashicbooks.com
www.akashicbooks.com

For my sister Teté,
my niece and nephews Susana, Enrique, and Eduardo,
and my dear friend Germán Blacut

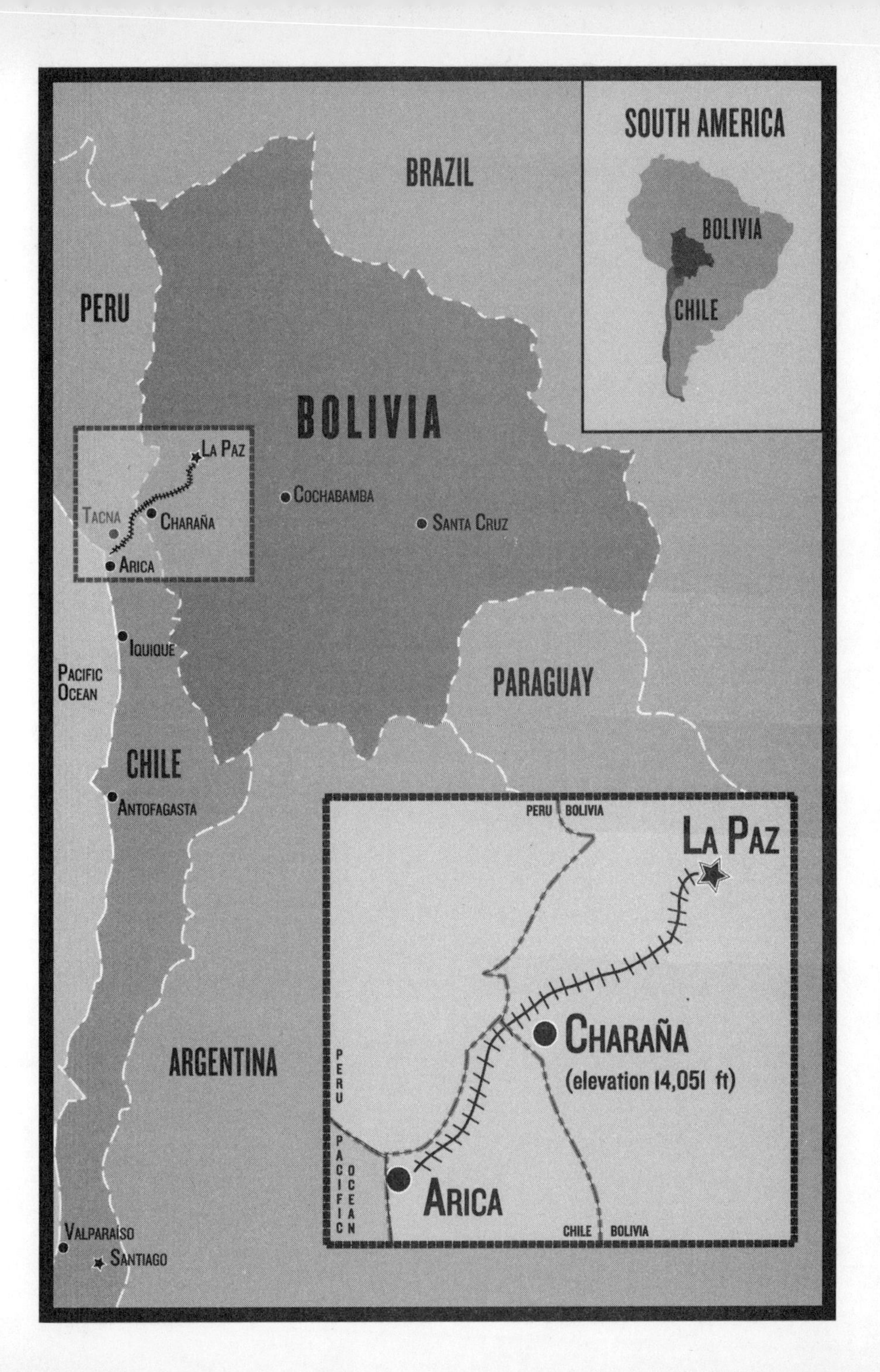
SOUTH AMERICA
BOLIVIA
CHILE
BRAZIL
PERU
BOLIVIA
La Paz
Tacna
Charaña
Arica
Cochabamba
Santa Cruz
Iquique
Pacific Ocean
PARAGUAY
CHILE
Antofagasta
ARGENTINA
Valparaíso
Santiago
PERU
BOLIVIA
La Paz
Charaña
(elevation 14,051 ft)
PERU
PACIFIC
OCEAN
Arica
CHILE
BOLIVIA

Ricardo Beintigoitia remembered perfectly that January morning in 1952. His best friend, Fat Fassell, had borrowed his father's black Chevrolet to take him to Central Station, where he would catch the train bound for Chile. The sun was shining and the sky was a deep blue, but you could still feel the morning chill. Fat Fassell opened the car's trunk, handed the suitcase to Ricardo, and lit an Astoria cigarette.

They entered the station and paused on the platform. Throngs of people were moving about: travelers, family members, newspaper and candy vendors, indigenous porters, policemen, and the odd vagrant who had come to watch the train pull away. Ricardo repeated the same ritual at the end of every school year. He had been traveling regularly to Arica since he was ten, usually in the company of his parents. This time, as Ricardo had just graduated from high school, his father had given him permission to enjoy a few days with his close friends, whom, after a few months' vacation, he might not see again for several years. Ricardo wanted to attend a university on the Old Continent. The previous night, members of his social club had organized a farewell party for him at the house of a wealthy friend, Judith, in Sopocachi. The boys drank until 3 in the morning and then hired a few taxis to take them to the Caiconi district. A gale-force wind pushed them toward a cluster of rustic bordellos and into the arms of call girls wasted from a long night of debauchery. At daybreak, accompanied by Fat Fassell, Ricardo headed to his house in San Jorge to pick up his luggage.

* * *

The locomotive sounded its first whistle, announcing that the slow, painful climb to El Alto would begin in twenty minutes. Fat Fassell exhaled a generous cloud of smoke from his Astoria, which had the effect of making everyone around him dizzy.

"I envy you, brother," Fassell said. "I'd give anything to see the ocean again."

"You'll be in Tubingen soon enough," Ricardo reminded him.

Fassell took another deep puff and scanned the horizon with a look of resignation.

"My ancestors, the Germans, are a pain in the ass. I would love to be a Bolivian until the day I die. After that I can be a German."

Fassell grabbed the suitcase and Ricardo followed him. The sleeping car was located at the very back of the train. A nervous-looking Indian boy, standing less than five feet tall and weighing no more than ninety pounds, approached and offered to help with the bag. The kid smiled, baring a set of teeth that resembled a weathered picket fence. After heaving the bag onto his back, he started jogging as if he were on a mountain trail. He stopped next to the car and placed the suitcase on the metal steps leading into the train.

A steward led the boys to the last cabin. He punched the ticket and asked, "Which one of you is traveling?"

"I am," Ricardo said.

"They're separating us. They know I'm bad news, a German jokester," Fassell said.

The steward declined Fassell's offer of an Astoria and explained that Ricardo would be sharing a cabin with a Franciscan priest. Sporting a gray uniform and a cap, his sterile appearance and diligent manner identified him as a prototypical Bolivian Railway employee. After knocking on the door to the cabin, the steward, apparently afraid of the priest, waited a few seconds before peering inside. With a seraphic smile, the priest let them in.

"Señor Beintigoitia will be joining you," the steward announced.

"I'll take the bottom bunk, if you don't mind," the priest said.

"It's all the same to me," Ricardo replied, placing his suitcase on the upper bunk.

They returned to the hallway. The steward looked at Ricardo with solicitous eyes. Ricardo took twenty pesos out of his pants pocket and placed them in the palm of his hand.

"Salvador Aldaviri, at your service," the man said. "The dining car will open as soon as we depart for El Alto."

Ricardo and Fat Fassell headed back to the platform. A half-breed woman wrapped in a heap of flowing skirts was selling sweets, and a shoeshine boy, dressed La Paz–style in a short vest and a cap, started to polish one of Fassell's boots without even asking.

"If I had a chick who could rub my balls like that, I'd be the happiest Teuton alive," Fassell said.

"I'll be back in two weeks," Ricardo said, ignoring his friend's comment. "Let's make plans to meet up in Europe."

"My dad wants to emigrate to Brazil," Fassell said. "He doesn't like what's happening in Bolivia. If it turns into anything like Argentina, we're screwed. Perón's a fascist and a populist, and he's trying to help the MNR take power. My dad wants to buy a ranch in São Paulo."

Fassell hugged Ricardo emphatically and left. Ricardo followed him with his eyes; his corpulence stood out amid the bustling crowd of silent, diminutive people dressed in black.

Ricardo reboarded the train. In the dining car, the waiters were busy cleaning tables, setting out tablecloths and glasses, arranging flower vases, and cleaning the windows with soap and water. The cooks could be seen lighting chunks of charcoal in army-size stoves and rinsing out gigantic metal pots. Next to the dining car were the second-class cars, crammed with poor people, nearly all of whom were smuggling crates of beer into Chile. At one end of the second car, a guy who looked like trouble, leaning against a wooden stool, watched Ricardo as he passed by. He looked about thirty years old and half his face was wrapped in a black scarf, revealing only his eyes, which were framed by thick brows and drooping lashes. Ricardo noticed that the man was holding a painter's easel.

Ricardo stepped off the train and walked past the freight cars, which had large, steel-clad interiors. Sweating indigenous freight handlers shouted at each other as they heaved large sacks of flour. A little man caked in white powder ordered them around. Ricardo recognized the engineer of the solid and shining English locomotive, which exhaled steam out its sides like an enormous bull gearing up for battle. It was Macario Quispe. An old-timer from Oruro, he was a veteran of that route, which climbed into the clouds before descending to the coast. His face, worn by the wind and the high-altitude sun, was a mask of bronze. Ricardo greeted him and the engineer responded with a slight nod. A couple of young coal men fed the train's belly.

"This engine is a Garrat," Ricardo said. "The English used them in India. No terrain is too much for them."

"The English know what a good locomotive is worth," Quispe responded.

Ricardo stroked the hot flank of the locomotive. He remembered the Uyuni train yard and the cold nights that he used to spend watching the trains coming and going. They hypnotized him and made him dream. They would transport him to distant, hostile lands, traversing snowy peaks perforated by countless tunnels in which magical colors suddenly appeared, making him tremble with delight. The vivid images from his childhood were so real he could almost touch them.

He retraced his steps and reentered the train. The late-arriving passengers boarded hastily, causing an uproar in the station. People could be heard shouting at the luggage boys to hurry up and nagging the indigenous porters, who were carrying gigantic loads on their backs and shoving them awkwardly through the windows. Ricardo glanced at the station clock: fifteen minutes until the train's departure. He recognized his uncle, Felipe Tréllez, harassing a tiny porter who was flattened under the weight of a huge trunk, and called to him.

"Hello," Tréllez said. "Are you done celebrating?"

"You only graduate from high school once."

"Which cabin are you in?"

"Number six. I'm sharing it with a Franciscan priest."

With a studied movement, Tréllez hopped onto the train. He was wearing a beige jacket, light gray pants, and, as usual, a felt hat. He was pushing forty, but looked younger. This may have been because he was thin and no more than 5'3", not to mention the splendid effect of the creams which softened his somewhat pale, wrinkle-free skin. His lean face and mocking expression made him look like a French colonist out of a Hollywood movie. A musketeer-style mustache lent him a frivolous air.

Moments later, Ricardo noticed the pompous figure of Alfredo Miranda, who was best known by his nickname, the Marquis. Miranda was the owner of the Tabarís, a popular cabaret. He had introduced full nudity to La Paz's dull strip clubs, bringing him renown and a tidy fortune, which he invested in hiring new girls from Chile. His 1930s

Don Juan silhouette was always on display at the Tabarís amid clouds of smoke, leaning against the bar, keeping an eye on the drunks, greeting the distinguished politicians, signaling to the waiters with a raise of the eyebrows, and tracking the movements of the girls as they entertained the clients. He was a pimp sui generis, a cross between Buenos Aires sleaze and La Paz affectation. Likable and snooty, he was famous for bedding all of the hostesses who worked in his bar.

Upon seeing Ricardo, the Marquis furrowed his speckled eyebrows and tried to recall some nocturnal encounter. At his side, a female companion followed him obediently. Like most passengers in the sleeping car, she had hired an indigenous porter, who was carrying a pair of leather suitcases which looked like they had been purchased from the shop of Gringo Freudenthal, a Jew who had escaped the Nazis.

Ricardo moved along to the tail end of the train. Next to the station gate, an autumnal elegant lady stood gazing at the platform. Behind her, a young woman wearing a red and blue plaid skirt and a white wool sweater walked slowly and half-heartedly.

"Tell your husband to hurry up," the older woman said loudly, putting exaggerated stress on the word "husband."

"Okay, okay," the young woman answered.

A dark-skinned, short-legged, paunchy man with graying hair blithely chased behind the young woman who was ordering her luggage boy to undo the rope that held together an impeccable set of American-style suitcases. Ricardo's eyes met those of the girl, his with a look of surprise and hers uneasy and embarrassed. The trio approached the sleeping car and ascended single file. Ricardo thought he had seen the young woman before, but he was unable to place her. As he transported himself to the past, someone raised the wooden blinds covering the window where he was standing. It was she, smiling at him uninhibitedly. When the dark-skinned man appeared at her side, her smile disappeared.

The final boarding call sounded and the second-class passengers made a mad dash for their respective cars. The train advanced a couple of yards and jerked abruptly, warning of its imminent departure.

Seconds later, the train began to roll. As Ricardo made his way back to his cabin, he saw a man rushing frantically, tripping over himself, struggling with a large bag. Curiously, the new arrival, although he was a relatively young fellow, was unable to grasp the handrail to climb up to the train. Ricado grabbed him by the arm and boosted him up the metal staircase in a swift motion. Panting, the man let the bag fall to the floor.

"You could have slipped and fallen under the wheels," Ricardo said.

"Thanks," the man replied. "The taxi I was riding in got a flat tire. I almost didn't make it." He then pointed at Ricardo with his index finger. "I know you. You always travel at this time of year. My name is Lalo Ruiz."

"Ruiz," Ricardo repeated without conviction.

"The poker player."

"Now I remember."

"You've grown a lot," Ruiz said.

"A few centimeters. Must be the swimming . . ."

Ruiz extended a sweaty hand. "Have you seen the other passengers?"

"Only a few of them. Why?"

"I'm looking for some fledglings to pluck. I'm not rich enough for vacations on the coast. I'm on this train to earn a few pesos."

"You have a long ride ahead of you. You're sure to find someone."

"Are you traveling with your parents?"

"No. They're waiting for me in Arica."

"Who are you rooming with?"

"A Franciscan priest."

"That's bad luck."

"I think the owner of the Tabarís is traveling with his wife."

"Wife? That guy is single. His wife left him in Valparaíso."

"I hardly know him."

"The Marquis is a nice guy but it's impossible to put one over on him. He's an old fox." Ruiz smiled. His yellow teeth had the ochre hue of nicotine. His eyes were slightly bloodshot. "I'll buy you a beer as soon as they open the dining car."

A steward led them down the corridor and knocked on the door of cabin two. A guy in short sleeves appeared. He was short and bald and his pants were held up with ratty suspenders. He was smoking a cigar.

"You are my roommate?" he asked.

Ruiz smirked, unamused by the encounter. He gave a miserly tip to the steward and said, "I'd like to introduce my friend Petko, a Russian loan shark who spends the entire day at the Club de La Paz café."

"Shit," the man exclaimed. "Of all people, is you. If I know, I take other train."

Ruiz fanned the cigar smoke with one hand and entered the cabin.

"I'm screwed," he said. "I'm gonna choke from that damn smoke."

"Tobacco, highest quality," mumbled Petko through his teeth. "I am screwed to listen to talk of bitter poker player."

Ruiz turned toward Ricardo. "What's your last name?"

"Beintigoitia."

"My friend, young Beintigoitia, whom I have had the pleasure of knowing for many years."

"You teach him to play poker?"

"He's a good kid. Not a degenerate like you."

Petko chewed on the end of his cigar with apparent satisfaction. Ricardo guessed that he was a little bit older than Ruiz. When he spoke Spanish, one could detect a marked Eastern European accent along with atrocious grammar. His facial features were not those of the typical Slavs whom Ricardo would see from time to time in Soviet films. He was beardless, he had no eyelashes or eyebrows, and his head was totally bald. He didn't seem to have ever possessed a single hair. He shone like a hardboiled egg coated with butter. Everything about him was small, except maybe his nose, which was not very big but stood out enough to lend his face a touch of extravagance.

"My name is Petko Danilov. I was born in city called Novgorod. Those communist bastards rename it Gorki. Do you know who is Gorki?"

"No idea."

"Boring novelist. Socialist realism. Writes about working class."

"I don't know much about Soviet literature."

"Good," Petko said. "I am Jewish, you know. In Bolivia some people are anti-Semites."

"I'm an anti-Semite," Ruiz said.

"Bull! You are nothing. Unlucky poker player. And bad loser too. Remember last time we played at Círculo Italiano? You almost start to cry."

Petko blew smoke in his face. Ruiz opened the window.

"I'll let you smoke until 5 in the afternoon. I don't want to die on the train."

Ricardo coughed.

"You see," Ruiz said, "your cigars are poisonous."

"That rich miner got on train," said Petko.

"Who?"

"He just married Carletti girl."

"Nazario Alderete?" asked Ruiz.

"Yes, yes, who else?"

Ruiz rubbed his hands. "He cheated me in a card game and made off with a piece of land I used to own in Achachicala."

"He is a card sharp," Petko said. "Now you can get your revenge."

Ricardo couldn't believe what he had just heard. He assumed it was a joke. After all, Jews were known for their sense of humor.

"That old guy I saw board the train is married to the girl with the plaid skirt?"

Petko sat down on the lower bunk. He took a handkerchief out of his pocket and wiped his forehead. "Heat in altitude unbearable," he said. "Yes . . . girl, daughter of late Carletti. I knew her father. He played bocce at Círculo Italiano. He knew how to cook pasta. He died when he lost mine in Potosí. They say that bastard take his money."

"How do you know all this?" Ruiz asked.

"At Club de La Paz you hear life and miracles of high society."

"That guy isn't high society. He just has money," Ruiz said.

"Money . . . and money rules."

"Not with a girl like that," Ricardo asserted.

"You are young; you do not know power of money." Petko drew a figure in the air as if to suggest something, but it wasn't clear what.

Ruiz was dressed in black; he looked like an undertaker. He took off his jacket, white shirt, and black tie and remained standing in his undershirt. Ricardo said he'd see them later.

The train left the station and climbed slowly through hills dotted with stands of eucalyptus en route to El Alto.

Back in his cabin, Ricardo watched the Franciscan unpack his scarce belongings. He was a bit surprised not to see, among his possessions, the traditional vestments used to celebrate Mass, such as the Holy Chasuble. The Franciscan placed on his bunk two shirts, a pair of pants, and a change of underwear. "My name is Daniel," he announced. "Father Daniel Moreno."

"Ricardo Beintigoitia. I just graduated from high school two weeks ago."

"Ready to begin life's journey," said Moreno.

Father Moreno didn't really look like a priest. He was too thickset and his mannerisms bore little resemblance to the simplicity and humility which characterized the followers of Saint Francis of Assisi.

"I wouldn't be able to sleep well on the top bunk. The slightest jolt and I could come falling down."

"There are safety belts to keep that from happening," said Ricardo.

"The English don't miss a thing. Bolivian Railway—doesn't it seem arrogant for a Bolivian company to have an English name, when the vast majority of people in this country are either indigenous or half-breeds like me?"

He was a man of medium height and had the build of a Turkish wrestler. His face, which was composed of unequal parts, nonetheless retained a certain harmony. His head was shaven except for a volcanic rim of hair, in the typical manner of the Chosen Ones.

"Do you snore?" the Reverend Father asked.

"Not that I know of."

Father Daniel looked at him for the first time with a certain curiosity. "Have you been a good student?"

"More or less."

"In the new Bolivia we're going to need talented and responsible people."

"The new Bolivia? And where do we leave the old one?"

Solemnly, Father Moreno lifted his jaw like a haughty llama. "Good question," he said.

Ricardo stepped out into the corridor. The train was continuing its climb through the trees. From time to time he glimpsed small dirt fields on which boys were playing soccer. Train-chasing dogs barked furiously at the passing locomotive. Before penetrating the tunnels which perforated the mountain, the engineer would yank a rope, unleashing a horn blast that broke the still air of that sunny morning.

The train's pace was lazy. The churning of the engine could be heard along with the sharp squeaking of the wheels as they snaked across the tracks. Suddenly, rounding a bend, a vista emerged of the city stretching down the valley toward the south. Clusters of shacks, forming the shantytowns, clung to the slopes of the mountain. It was an unusual spectacle that hypnotized the passengers. Ricardo, who traveled this route every year, took note of how La Paz was growing without order, skirting precipices, reaching for the mountain tops.

The girl he had seen earlier in the station hurried out of the cabin next to his and slammed the door. She seemed irritated. Her pearly cheeks were burning; she looked like she had just been subjected to a lava bath. She rested both hands on the windowsill and turned her uneasy gaze toward him.

"I think we know each other from somewhere," Ricardo said.

"I have the same impression," she replied.

"I'm Ricardo Beintigoitia."

"Gulietta Carletti."

"Is it okay if I call you *tú*?"

"Of course."

"You're quite flushed. Is something wrong?"

"Nothing serious. Just a little dizzy."

"A cup of coca tea would do the trick."

The door to Carletti's cabin opened and the husband's insolent figure injected itself between them.

"I'll be damned, you already have company," he said with sarcasm.

Gulietta threw a punch at him with her eyes.

"I want to speak with you for a moment," the man said.

She had no choice but to obey him. Alderete looked Ricardo over from head to toe. His smile was hateful, like the sneer of a Gestapo guard.

Ricardo dodged his oversized buttocks and headed toward the dining car. It was nearly empty. The poker player had settled in at a table near the kitchen. When he saw Ricardo, he invited him to sit down. His hands, covered with moles and warts, were shuffling a deck of cards. He ordered a round of beers.

"Waiting for your first victim?"

"It's still very early. I'm just massaging them. It's a matter of friendship. Later, they'll respond to me."

Lalo Ruiz made his living from poker. Railroad dining cars were his specialty. He traveled constantly, ripping off unwitting enthusiasts. He was an addict who needed not only to win, but to lose as well.

The fun of it lay in that perpetual disequilibrium, in the day-to-day instability.

"How's the Reverend Father?"

"A bit of a curmudgeon."

"It's not bad to have a friar at your side. Don't forget that we'll be reaching an elevation of around 16,000 feet."

"I've known you ever since I could talk," said Ricardo.

"That's true. I spend my life on trains. This dining car is a great place for trapping idiots."

He was right. The dining car of the La Paz–Arica train was the perfect environment for confounding occasional gamblers. The roar of the train, the misery of the Altiplano, the desire to see the ocean: All of this produced an uncontrollable yearning for entertainment, and what better way to get it than playing cards with the conjurer of that journey through the clouds.

"The Marquis plays poker?" asked Ricardo.

"When he's got nothing else to do. He trades in dancers whom he brings from Chile, and I figure he's on his way to see the goods in person. He has a sharp eye. The woman traveling with him is Anita Romero, the most famous madam in the country. She's Chilean. She plays go-between; years ago, she ran a couple of brothels in Caiconi. Don't tell me you never went there."

Ricardo blushed.

Ruiz wasn't impressed and continued: "There was no resisting it. Now she's old and retired from the business. As an advisor she's a gold mine."

"I'd like you to play that Alderete guy and destroy him."

"You don't like him?"

"If I'm not mistaken, the guy's an asshole."

"You're not mistaken. He's the biggest asshole of them all."

"Petko said you should ask him for a rematch."

"I'll challenge him," said Ruiz. "If he lets me, I promise you that he'll never forget this trip."

Ruiz asked for something to snack on. The train entered a tunnel, causing the water to disappear in the darkness. The waiter returned with a plate of peanuts and French fries. Ruiz was in a good mood. An insouciant smile lit up his face, which looked like that of a bird of prey. Ricardo couldn't help but admire his simple happiness, unbounded by the inscrutable mysteries of life. The poker player was a born optimist, the kind whose enthusiasm is contagious.

"Here comes that Alderete's wife," Ruiz said.

Gulietta settled into a table in the middle of the car. She was alone and she began to contemplate the landscape. Off in the distance, Mount Illimani's magnificence was on full display. Evanescent clouds adorned its snowy peaks. Ricardo thanked Ruiz for the beer and approached Gulietta.

"May I sit down?"

"Of course. Did my husband say anything to you?"

"He didn't have time," Ricardo said. "Now I remember where we saw each other. In Buenos Aires, at my aunt Blanca Colorado's house."

"It's possible," Gulietta said. "I studied in Buenos Aires. I just graduated."

"Me too," Ricardo said. "From the Instituto Americano."

"Blanca Colorado. Isn't she the poet?"

"Exactly."

The irritated expression that Ricardo remembered from the corridor had vanished. Her face, though not beautiful, was attractive. Her eyes, which looked as if they had matured before her other features, gazed indolently at her surroundings with a bold sensuality.

She summoned the waiter and asked for a cup of black coffee.

"I imagine you already know that I'm married to Alderete."

"It surprised me," Ricardo said, trying not to sound imprudent.

"Someday I'll explain it to you."

The waiter placed the coffee on the table and walked away.

She took off her shoes, bending down without taking her eyes off Ricardo. He felt her foot brush against his ankle.

"I'd like to ask you to give me a foot massage, but that would be too forward."

"In the end," Ricardo said, "we're from the same generation and we play the same games."

Gulietta caressed the sides of the cup. Her long, fine fingers wrapped around it in a tactile ceremony.

"I bet you're dying to know how a woman like me married an old half-breed like Alderete."

"Maybe you're in love."

"Don't be ridiculous. Love is blind, but even the blind have a sense of touch."

"Then tell me."

"You might misunderstand. It's a complicated story. Let's talk about you. When my mom saw you, she told me she's friendly with your parents. She also warned me that you would try to make a move on me."

Ricardo smiled. "What else did she tell you?"

"That you're a goof-off. That you hang out with those boys from Saint George's."

"They've been my buddies since grade school."

"They drink a lot."

"Only beer."

"At the Chic café on Rosendo Gutiérrez."

"How do you know so much?"

"La Paz is a small town. Who are you going out with?"

"I don't have a steady girlfriend."

"How strange. There are lots of pretty girls."

"Most of them are a little too old-fashioned."

"And you don't like that?"

"Let's say that it makes me feel inhibited."

"At the Instituto Americano they teach American Lit, I suppose."

"No, that would have been great, but instead they overloaded us with grammar. Even so, that was my most interesting class . . . the teacher was pretty hot."

"My mother's right. You're not a very serious person." Gulietta drank the rest of her coffee, stood up, and looked around furtively at her surroundings. She walked away, swaying her compact, fluid hips.

The train was drawing close to the El Alto district. On the edge of the cliff, which marked the beginning of the endless plateau, the first shacks were discernible. A whistle announced that the train was reaching the end of its climb. The dining car emptied out, its passengers making way for the waiters setting tables for lunch, which would be served once the train left El Alto. The sun was shining gloriously. An expanse of trees, which had been planted recently to humidify the extremely dry air, moved to the rhythm of a dusty wind. The green patch tinged the pale mountain. The curves of the train tracks, which were cut into the mountainside and hung over the abyss like a series of balconies, disappeared as the land turned flat and the horizon became one with the sky.

On the platform of the El Alto station lay piles of bundled coca leaves. Ricardo spotted a few stragglers who had probably missed the train at Central Station in La Paz and hired a taxi to catch up in El

Alto, which would be an easy feat, since it took the train an hour to reach its first stop whereas a taxi made the trip in thirty minutes.

A blond-haired man weighing well over two hundred pounds commanded a porter to load luggage into the sleeping car in a hurry. To Ricardo, the leather coat in which the man was wrapped evoked a German military officer from the Second World War. The man led a woman by the hand who was dressed completely in black and wore a hat that looked like a bullfighter's cap covered with fine gauze. The railway inspector approached the man and greeted him deferentially. He then greeted the woman and helped them both up onto the train. Ricardo noticed three eccentric-looking women holding their skirts as they battled the wind. The most attractive one, a contortionist for a Chilean circus troupe that often visited Bolivia, had a puppy on her lap. Next to her was a midget with an enormous head that looked as if it belonged in a pumpkin contest, laughing uncontrollably in concert with the third woman, who had the unmistakable look of a gypsy. She was wearing a red headscarf and a long skirt which brushed against the small cement platform. The contortionist tried going up the ramp with the puppy on her back until the inspector shouted, "No dogs allowed on board!"

"And where do you want me to put him?" the woman shot back.

"In the freight car," the inspector said.

"If he can't travel, then I won't either."

The gypsy and the midget joined in the ruckus. The Franciscan opened one of the train windows and the contortionist approached the car pouting, holding back tears. After they exchanged a few words, the priest promptly descended the walkway and planted himself in front of the inspector.

"The cold in Charaña will be too much for him. He'll die," Father Moreno said.

"We can't break company rules," the inspector replied emphatically.

Father Moreno adopted a monastic tone. The inspector, who had been raised in the English tradition, didn't budge.

"Saint Francis taught us to love animals," Father Moreno said in a deliberate, artificial-sounding voice.

"I love dogs too, but I won't let one travel in a passenger car."

"So what can I do?" the contortionist asked.

"Like I told you, you'll have to leave it in a freight car. You've got no other choice."

"That's an absurd rule," she said.

"That's just the way it is. I don't make the rules around here."

"It's a puppy," Father Moreno argued. "It's not a Saint Bernard."

"A dog is a dog," the man averred.

The gypsy stepped in. "You just don't listen. You're being stubborn."

"And rude," the midget added.

"Lower your voice!" demanded the inspector.

A crewman opened one of the freight cars and the contortionist deposited her dog.

"It's too hot in there," Father Moreno said. "The dog's going to fry."

"Which one is it going to be," the inspector said, "death from cold or death from heat?"

"What a jerk!" the contortionist exclaimed.

"I suppose that once it gets dark, they could open the car and bring him a blanket," Father Moreno suggested.

"We'll see," the inspector answered.

As the train slowly pulled away from the station, the gypsy and the midget waved goodbye with their handkerchiefs. The contortionist settled into one of the second-class cars.

Alderete walked out into the corridor wearing an undershirt, his mud-colored torso looking as smooth as a newborn baby's. "What's going on?"

"Something about a dog," the priest said.

Alderete scrutinized him like a policeman sizing up a crook. "Your face is familiar," he said.

"We Franciscans look alike, maybe because of our modest appearance."

Alderete frowned. "You look exactly like a rabble-rouser I know who's always inciting the mineworkers to rise up with the MNR* against the owners."

Father Moreno turned slightly pale. "They say we all have a double somewhere," he said, his voice trailing off.

**The leftist Movimiento Nacionalista Revolucionario (Nationalist Revolutionary Movement) spearheaded a popular revolution in Bolivia in 1952.*

The train left the El Alto district and traveled deep into the Andean plateau. Tiny mud and straw huts were scattered across the countryside, which grew increasingly barren as the city was left farther and farther behind. By the time Ricardo entered the dining car, nearly every table had been taken. The better-off second-class passengers congregated around the snack counter. In exchange for a few pesos, the waiter led Ricardo to a table with two chairs. Ricardo settled in, looked around, and noticed a table marked *Reserved* in the middle of the car. It was probably for the Alderetes. Ricardo was intrigued and wanted to know more about Gulietta and her strange marriage. She had introduced him to her world and he wanted to be part of it, at least for the duration of the twenty-four-hour trip.

The remaining guests from the sleeping car continued to arrive. As was to be expected, they had changed clothes for the occasion. Ricardo's uncle, Pepe Tréllez, was sporting a brown suit, white shirt, striped tie, and Panama hat. When he saw that Ricardo was alone, he went to join him.

"You're looking good," Tréllez said.

"It's the thought of traveling to the coast."

"Did you pass with flying colors?"

"Not really."

"Well, what matters is that you passed."

Pepe Tréllez was wearing too much cologne. He reeked like a high-class chorus girl. Assessing his next move, like an actor before a mirror, he eyed the other passengers with an air of superiority. "There's nobody worth going for."

"The Carletti girl," Ricardo said.

Tréllez smiled. His brown eyes, ever in search of surprises, looked amusedly at Ricardo. "Do you know the story?"

"No. But I can imagine."

"It's no soap opera. It's more like one of those depressing Vargas Vila books."

The Marquis was letting himself be seen with Anita. He had on a blue suit, a light blue shirt, and a wild green and yellow–splashed tie that resembled a slice of the jungle. Anita—La Paz's most famous madam—was wearing a girlish pink dress and looked like a doll out of a nightmare.

"The Marquis puts too much powder on his face. He thinks life is one long cabaret."

"The poker player told me Anita is a madam."

"She's the most experienced one," Tréllez said. "She was very beautiful until just a few years ago. She knows everyone in La Paz."

A waiter cleared a table for four next to the kitchen where some railway employees had been sitting. He invited the Marquis to sit down.

"How have you been, Pepe?" the Marquis said in greeting.

"Worried," Tréllez replied.

"Why?"

"My Indian farmhands are getting riled up over all this Marxist bullshit."

"Sell your land before the holocaust."

The Marquis was waiting for the man and the woman Ricardo had seen on the El Alto station platform. As the couple entered the car, they recognized Pepe Tréllez and waved. The man was wearing a light green tweed jacket, khaki pants, and boots.

"That's Ian Durbin, an Irishman who works for the Bolivian Railway. The quiet, sad-looking woman is his wife. She's from Potosí."

"Durbin is huge," Ricardo said.

"He weighs around 220 pounds. In his younger days in Dublin, I think he was a boxer. The guy is a serious drinker. He can finish off a bottle of whiskey in half an hour by himself."

The waiter placed two bowls of *chairo* soup on the table and asked: "Anything to drink?"

"A beer," Tréllez said. "Do they let you drink beer?"

"I'm eighteen," Ricardo said.

"How time flies. I remember when you used to ride that tricycle around your house on Federico Zuazo."

Tréllez poured hot sauce into his soup. "Here comes Alderete. Poor girl. To have to put up with a pig like him."

Alderete couldn't hide the angry grimace etched on his dark face.

"The one behind the girl is her mother," Tréllez explained. "Doña Clara is from La Paz's crème de la crème. She arranged the marriage."

"Really?"

"Alderete cheated her late husband out of his mine. He was the guy's accountant."

Doña Clara was the image of simplicity. Half her body was wrapped in a gray shawl. Gulietta was wearing a bluish skirt and a fine sweater of braided wool. She turned her gaze on Ricardo and caught him staring at her, spellbound.

"She's really beautiful," Ricardo said.

"And they say she's smart. What do you think of the trio, nephew?"

"A permanent short circuit."

"I've always admired brave women, like Isabella of Castile and the

Coronilla heroines*," Tréllez said. "But anyone who can put up with that guy deserves to be canonized."

"You don't seem to think much of him."

"He's a son of a bitch," Tréllez said in English.

The languid whistle of the locomotive sounded, announcing its arrival at a tiny village near an ancient-looking farmhouse. Alderete's hoarse and heavy voice was the only other dissonant noise, aside from the cars' incessant swaying from side to side. The train stopped in front of a small stone house covered by a red corrugated-metal roof.

A thin, bony man rang a bell heralding the train's arrival. Behind the building, at the end of a windy path, there was a farmyard in which a group of skinny cows rested alongside a small bull swatting flies with its tail. A solitary dog barked half-heartedly.

Ricardo was surprised by the sight of the contortionist walking deliberately alongside the train, toward the car in which her dog had been confined. The railway inspector followed behind her, talking to the wind. The station manager joined them, apparently unaware of what was happening. The contortionist touched the side of the car with one hand and cried out in pain.

"It's an oven in there. My dog must be suffocating from the heat."

The inspector released a heavy lock and slid open the iron gate. The contortionist called out to her dog, which was named Sulfo.

"This is the last time I'll open it before Charaña," the inspector said.

Sulfo was alive, but dehydrated. The heat had weakened him so much that it was painful for him to bark.

"I'll complain to the authorities," the contortionist said.

"We are the authorities," the inspector replied. "Enough of your complaints."

**On May 27, 1812, a group of women and children mounted a last-ditch attempt to prevent the seizure of the city of Cochabamba, Bolivia by forces loyal to Spain on a hilltop called "La Coronilla."*

The station manager produced a bucket of water and the mutt drank until he was satisfied.

The rustic silhouette of Father Moreno soon appeared. It was not exactly a divine apparition; he looked more like a well-fed medieval cleric. He ambled along the dry, hard ground, patting his bulky paunch.

"Father, you seem to appear every time this lady is making a fuss," the railway man said.

"I have a way of calming people down. How's the little dog, Carla Marlene?"

"How do you think he is!"

The engineer broke the high-mountain silence and the locomotive sent a shudder through the line of cars. The Andean plain provided the only stretch where the train could reach a velocity of more than fifty kilometers per hour. Here and there, haciendas surrounded by green fields and grazing cattle appeared. Peasant huts were scattered throughout the surrounding area. Train-chasing dogs were in abundance, and even tiny, fleet-footed pigs occasionally joined the pursuit. There could not have been a more auspicious beginning to the afternoon: a clear blue sky and, on the horizon, reddish mountains. The air was clean and the sun painted an amber hue across the empty steppe. Ricardo lit a cigarette and Pepe Tréllez packed a pipe as they waited for their coffee.

"I don't see that Russian guy Petko around," Ricardo said.

"He'll eat later. He doesn't like crowds."

"He's a funny guy."

"He's loaded," Tréllez said. "He's the banker for all the Jews in La Paz."

"He told me Alderete's a crook."

"He's right. Alderete screwed me over once and he's going to pay for it. I'm waiting for the right moment. I'm a civilized guy but I crack if anyone touches my womenfolk."

"Aunt Graciela?"

"No . . . no . . . no one bothers Graciela, not even drunks."

"Then who are you talking about?"

"You're a curious one, nephew. First let me tell you something about the Carletti family."

Pepe Tréllez's pipe was shaped like a seahorse. He lit it and watched the smoke rise to the ceiling.

"Alderete belongs to the PURS*. He's an active Ballivián supporter, just like the other mine owners. Up until a few years ago, he was just an accountant at a tin mine owned by Rafael Carletti, Gulietta's father, a guy from Genoa who emigrated to Bolivia after the First World War. With his money from Italy, Carletti bought himself a mine in Potosí on the cheap from a Croat who had worked it unsuccessfully. It wasn't too large, but the mine was big enough to provide a good living. Alderete worked with him for a few years without a problem. Carletti was an elegant, sophisticated fellow. He was good-looking, and one fine day, at a ranch in Río Abajo, he met Doña Clara, who is from one of the best families in La Paz. They married a few months later. They had just one daughter and they named her Gulietta. They led a regular bourgeois life, owned a beautiful home in Sopocachi, and traveled every year to Buenos Aires. Society life in La Paz, if you have money, is not bad. It can be a very pleasant city; the people are civilized and they have an enviable sense of humor. Everything was going great until our Italian friend met a woman from Potosí, the daughter of an Austrian man and a woman from Chuquisaca, during one of his nights on the town. He fell for her their first night together. People who knew the girl—her name was Tomasita—say that

**Spanish initials for the Socialist Republican Union Party, a coalition of right-wing parties that supported a military takeover in 1951 under the rule of General Hugo Ballivián.*

she sucked him dry like a stalk of sugar cane. She was a human sponge.

"Carletti stopped going to the mine," Tréllez continued, "and left everything in the hands of his accountant, Alderete. He dedicated himself to copulating as if his life depended on it. The half-breed girl drove him crazy. He bought her a house and a car. Since she didn't know how to drive, Carletti hired a chauffeur and the guy ended up bedding her. The two of them fled to Venezuela together. Carletti started drinking heavily, and by the time he bothered checking up on the mine again, it was about to be foreclosed. Alderete had forged Carletti's signature and taken out a million-dollar loan from the bank. Instead of using that credit to work the mine, the little accountant acquired property in La Paz in his cousin's name. On the verge of losing the mine, Carletti sold it for pennies to a guy who turned out to be a pawn of Alderete's. He went home to La Paz with little more than the shirt on his back.

"Doña Clara, who spent all her time back then playing rummy, listened to his entire confession one night and forgave him. Carletti forgot about Tomasa's thighs but he wasn't able to lay off the booze. He turned into a high-class vagrant and died of cirrhosis. Gulietta was at his side until the very end."

While telling the story, Tréllez didn't once take his eyes off Alderete, who was stuffing himself with peanuts.

"Doña Clarita went through difficult times at first, but she toughened up with the passing months. She had sworn to get revenge on Alderete, but didn't know how. The opportunity began to present itself when she bumped into him at the Max Bieber café. Gulietta was with her. It was the fatal moment for Alderete. Just as the late Genovese guy had hitched up with the lady from Potosí, the social-climbing Alderete had fallen like a schoolboy for Gulietta's good looks. No one knows the details of how they arranged the marriage, but Doña Clara did benefit from it financially."

"And Alderete didn't go to prison for forging the signature?" Ricardo asked.

"The Bolivian justice system is truly blind," Tréllez said.

"Poor girl."

"Alderete and Gulietta got a house in Obrajes and a pension for Doña Clara. They just got married. This is their honeymoon."

"And why did they bring the old lady along?"

"She's not so old. A night with her wouldn't be such a sacrifice," Tréllez said. "I imagine it's part of the arrangement; leaving Gulietta alone with that gargoyle would be dangerous."

"I still don't understand how Doña Clara could sacrifice her daughter like that," Ricardo said.

"You're too young to understand these things," Tréllez replied, signaling the end of the story.

The train slowed to a crawl; a pack of llamas was crossing the tracks. Despite the shouts of the peasant who was herding them, the animials blocked the train's path and paid no attention to the blaring horn. The train had to wait until the last llama had passed over the railroad tracks.

As the train resumed its forward march, the waiters began serving in the dining car. During lunch, Gulietta and Ricardo exchanged glances. Her glances were not casual ones; rather, they seemed to seek him out. Ricardo didn't know what to think. An erection that had begun as a light tickle was taking shape. Within minutes, he was at the mercy of the pole stuck inside his pants. Never before had a society girl turned him on like that with a simple stare. Using his left hand, he straightened out his "little friend" and trapped it with his belt.

"Is something wrong?" asked Tréllez.

"It's nothing, uncle."

"You look strange."

"It's the altitude."

"You think I'm stupid, don't you?"

"Not at all, uncle."

"Some people think I'm absentminded, but I do notice details. It's the Carletti girl. She's getting to you, isn't she?"

"I can't hide anything from you."

"I can hear your heart beating."

"She's married and she's on her honeymoon."

"Let's call it a total lunar eclipse. It's best not to see that guy at night."

The waiter left the bill and smiled routinely.

"This one's on me," Tréllez said. "You'll buy me a cognac at the Hotel Pacífico in Arica." He then stood up and sauntered over to Alderete's table. Gulietta and Doña Clara looked up while the ex-accountant, who was drinking coffee, remained oblivious to Pepe Tréllez's silent presence. He took off his hat, bowed Japanese-style, and said: "Gulietta, allow me to congratulate you on your marriage."

Doña Clarita smiled uncomfortably. Gulietta simply looked away. Alderete had not seen a ghost from his past in a long time. Once he noticed Tréllez, his mop of hair stiffened.

"I think you'd best be on your way, back to those French broads you love to pimp," Alderete said.

Pepe Tréllez was a gentleman raised in the age-old tradition of chivalry and good manners. Upon hearing these words, he went cold and turned pale. A few seconds passed in absolute silence. The waiters stopped making their rounds and the cooks ceased their pot banging.

Tréllez passed through every color in the rainbow before his skin turned a cherry hue. "How dare you speak to me like that; you're nothing but a prick who steals mines!"

Alderete abruptly stood up, but Doña Clara was seated between him and Tréllez. He asked her permission to hit him. This pause would prove fatal. Tréllez seized the moment and slapped Alderete twice in the face, leaving him speechless and overwhelmed by a strange inertia. A roar of laughter arose from the corner where Durbin, the Marquis, and the poker player were sitting.

"Sit down, don't pay any attention to him," Doña Clara advised.

"He's embarrassed," Alderete stammered. "Years ago, when he was the ambassador in Paris, he brought a French girl back with him and hid her in his pad on Seis de Agosto, near San Jorge. His wife caught them in the act."

Alderete sat down. His initial bewilderment gave way to an expression of satisfied revenge. A forced smile deformed his swollen peasant face.

Tréllez leaned over the table and muttered: "What your wife doesn't know is that once you realized you couldn't win over the French girl, even with all your stolen money, you sent a handwritten note to my wife telling her everything, including the address of the apartment."

That was enough for Gulietta and Doña Clara. They stepped away from the scene of battle.

"Poor girl, so removed from reality," Durbin said in English, in a voice like that of a Shakespearean actor.

The car emptied in no time at all. The passengers traveling second class surely thought it was a problem between "gentlemen" and headed for the exit. The laughter continued at Durbin's table as someone yelled, "Way to go, Don Pepe!"

Alderete's anger was building up like a boiler without a pressure valve. He felt a sharp pain in his stomach and an uncontainable rush of gases. He was on the verge of letting loose the loudest fart in the history of the La Paz–Arica train line; that would be his revenge. He stood up and pointed to his derrière.

Standing in the center of the car with his arms crossed, Tréllez smiled tauntingly. The gases played a mean trick on Alderete. Instead of exiting, they went straight up and pressed against a heart already tormented by rage. They imprisoned it like the tentacles of a giant octopus. He grew short of breath, and at that altitude, finding extra oxygen was highly unlikely. Gripping the seat backs, Alderete left the dining car and moved down the hallway to his cabin. He banged on the door repeatedly. Nobody answered.

"I'm choking," he said. "Gulietta . . . where are you?"

The steward helped him inside. Alderete collapsed on top of his bunk. Several minutes later, Gulietta came by to see what was happening.

Alderete looked at her with his eyes wide open. He was breathing with difficulty through his mouth and he clutched her shoulder with one hand. "A glass of water," he begged.

Gulietta took a pitcher from the counter and poured water into a glass.

"I have high blood pressure," Alderete said. "I don't handle these blowups well."

Doña Clara appeared, looking as calm as a nun strolling through a park.

"I'll tell Ricardo to look for a doctor in second class," Gulietta said.

Alderete let out a groan. Doña Clara unbuttoned his shirt and put her ear to his chest.

* * *

There was a wide range of odors in second class despite the country air that penetrated the few open windows. Ricardo saw construction workers, contraband dealers, carpenters, and illegal immigrants, but a doctor was nowhere to be found. At the end of the second car, an apprentice nurse headed for Santiago turned up. She was seventeen years old and was only trained to give injections. Alderete would have to fend for himself.

Ricardo asked if anyone knew if they were near any big towns. He didn't recognize any of the names. Someone suggested a cup of coca tea and even a suppository. Ricardo looked around and saw a disheveled, bearded painter with the eyes of an insomniac. His face was brimming with annoyance. A greasy mane fell over his shoulders.

"Is he Chilean or Bolivian?" the man asked.

"The sick guy? What does it matter?"

The painter smirked.

On his way back through the dining car, Ricardo heard Durbin remark, "The guy's got nine lives, like a cat."

"It takes something extra to kill someone like him," Tréllez said.

The sun was beating down hard. The Altiplano* looked like a desert on fire. The only shadows came from solitary trees rimming the walls of the peasant huts.

Ricardo found Gulietta in the dining car. "There's no doctor," he said.

"He's already better. It's pure theater. He just wants to impress me."

Ricardo touched her hand. Since she made no effort to pull away, he began caressing it, at first softly, and then he clasped both his hands around it.

"In Buenos Aires you could have asked me out to the movies," Gulietta said.

**The high Andean plateau extending through portions of Bolivia, Peru, Chile, and Argentina.*

"An animated film? We were too young back then."

Gulietta stroked his chest. Ricardo was sporting a fashionable, loose-fitting New York–style shirt. It was impossible to stay indifferent to her barely perceptible touch.

"I don't know what I'm going to do," Gulietta said.

"With Alderete?"

"He's my husband."

"Why did you marry him?"

She was silent. She was caught in a whirlwind of emotion. Her beautiful brown eyes teared up. "Poverty scares me more than death," she finally said.

"Some of the other travelers don't exactly respect your husband. Tréllez says this trip is like your lunar eclipse."

She laughed, which made her look even lovelier. She was a captivating girl. Her parents were European, but her genes seemed to have skipped a generation: She was dark-haired, of medium height, slender, and very feminine. Her skin was olive-toned, like that of an upper-class woman from India. Her body was harmonious; there was a delicate sensuality about her. Ricardo was under the impression that, up until then, her life had passed by as if it were a dream, like water flowing down a river without whirlpools or rocks to disturb its tranquility. But Gulietta had not recovered from the shock of her sudden impoverishment and her marriage to her father's ex-accountant, a man she disdained.

Ricardo wasn't sure her character was strong enough to put up with Alderete for long. The humiliation of being at the beck and call of the bean counter was probably an unbearable punishment.

"I have to go check on him," Gulietta said. "I'll see you later."

Ricardo liked the girl, but he knew that train romances nearly always ended abruptly and prematurely. This would be no exception; besides, Gulietta was traveling with her husband, who, having survived an acute episode of high blood pressure, was going to be just fine. In any event, part of the afternoon had already passed, then night would come, and the following day, in a matter of hours, they would be on the Chilean coast.

It wasn't like the Paris-Istanbul or the Trans-Siberian line, where the trip lasts nearly a week and relationships have time to begin, develop, and find reason for hope upon arriving at their destination. The affair between Captain Vronsky and Anna Karenina began on a train and continued until the curtain call in Moscow. If it had happened on the La Paz–Arica line, the game would have been over for Vronsky. Timing is everything. Ricardo was at the age where it made sense to either rush into a sexual adventure—a casual tryst that would just as soon be forgotten—or pursue the classic courtship of a girl of his social standing, which generally involved a degree of mutual attraction and the occasional absentminded caress, and no more.

He understood that it would be nearly impossible to make a move on her, even if the circumstances were favorable; furthermore, the naïve bourgeois flirting game was absurd and would only end up frustrating him. Ricardo decided to let destiny play Cupid. He didn't hold out much hope, but his gut told him that something unexpected could occur.

Edmundo Rocha woke with a start, sweating. With his left hand, he reached for a flask of *pisco* on the floor and took a long swig. For years, he had done nothing but drink *pisco* and sometimes pure alcohol, the kind that's sold in cans and intended for hardcore vagrants. Despite an overwhelming desire to finish it off, he left the bottle on top of the chair next to his bed. He lit a cigarette and sat up. He was wearing striped underpants that had been cut out from an old pair of pajamas. The stump that was his left leg stuck out grotesquely, shamefully. Rocha stared at it for a good while. He was alone in the cabin; the upper bunk was undisturbed. He knew that nobody would occupy it because he had two tickets in his jacket pocket: He had bought an extra one so that nobody would bother him.

As usual, he had been dreaming and his dream had turned into a nightmare, the same one as always. It used to happen at night, but lately it had begun plaguing him during siestas and post-binge sleepiness. The visions had a spine-chilling clarity to them. They would start with the cursed scene of him descending into the mine shaft on the ore car and then continue as he penetrated deeper into the mine. The naked torsos of his fellow workers were mirrors in which his own anguished face, his mop of hair, and his long, disheveled beard were reflected. He wanted to get out of the car, as it increasingly became one with the darkness and the silence, but it was impossible to move. His legs didn't respond and when he tried to shout, his throat went dry like a desert sandpit. There was nothing to be done. An evil force was leading him to the thick rock, which he was supposed to blow up with dynamite. His sweaty hands grasped the dynamite stick while Alcón, his mine buddy, chipped away at the rock with a pick. Alcón was making strange noises that sounded like wails. When he determined that the dynamite had been inserted deep enough into the rocky wall, he lit a match and they both started to run. The nightmare would pause there, with him escaping in slow motion. Then the other nightmare would begin, the one Rocha would see while waking up. The subsoil was slippery, the sticky underbelly of a mountain suffering at the hands of men tearing apart its insides. Rocha was desperately stumbling and falling. He would try to pull himself up, but he had lost time. No sooner did he succeed in standing up, than he heard the boom of the explosion and the burning gust propelled him several yards forward. Alcón shouted and pointed to the arch above, which was coming undone in thick and rough sheets of rock that were crashing down on both his legs. He managed to save his right leg, but his left leg got jammed under an enormous rock, turning it into a gelatinous, irrecoverable mass.

It's all that asshole's fault. If he hadn't sent me into the mines, I'd still be standing on two legs.

Rocha placed the crutches under his armpits and started to move from one side of the cabin to the other. Someone knocked on the door. The slightest noise could provoke a certain desperation in him.

"Who is it?"

"I have your lunch."

Rocha opened the door and let the waiter enter.

"One *chairo* soup, one large plate of meat, and a cup of applesauce."

"What time is it?"

"One o'clock, señor. You said you wanted the late lunch."

"Right . . . right," Rocha said, then handed the waiter a tip and closed the door.

He ate the soup and devoured the meat and accompanying French fries. As he savored the dessert, he thought again about his tragedy.

My nightmares end tonight. Once I take him out, I'll go back to sleeping like I used to. I'll sleep for hours and I'll dream about quiet lakes and beautiful eyes that love me. About the lush forests of Beni and rivers that look like the sea. All the things I lost because of that bastard—

Moments later, another knock on the door. It was the waiter coming to retrieve the tray.

"Can I get you anything else?"

"No . . . nothing," Rocha said. "I'm going to rest."

"Are you all right?"

"I have a fever," Rocha lied. "But I'm sure that tomorrow, on the coast, I'll feel better."

"There's nothing like being on the coast," the waiter said, and disappeared.

Rocha lay down. It was cold and his stump hurt. Sharp, stabbing pain shot up and down his leg. He rubbed the affected area with some ointment, then propped his head on a pillow and tried to picture Alderete, just as he was the day he went to visit the guy in the mining company office to ask him for a job. Alderete was his half-brother. They shared the same mother, an indigenous woman who had been the lover of Nazario's father. Edmundo's father was a carpenter from Oruro who died of a lung infection. Before succumbing to a terminal illness, his mother had advised Rocha to visit his half-brother, who seemed to have a good thing going in the mineral trade. He was an accountant and handled a lot of money. Rocha, who was going through hard times, had become little more than a drunken hobo who wandered from one place to another selling textiles and other odds and ends. He didn't think twice, and as soon as he had collected a few pesos, he headed for Potosí. Alderete worked in an office downtown in a well-preserved two-story building. At first he refused to see Rocha, claiming that he was too busy with work; however, several days later, upon noticing Rocha sitting in the lobby, he decided it would be better to attend to him once and for all and be done with it. Rocha showed him a letter from his mother and a few photographs of Nazario at the age of seven. Alderete read the missive and looked at him with a certain curiosity mixed with arrogance.

"So you're my half-brother. You look really bad."

"Things are tough over in Caracoles."

"I can imagine."

"Our mother is very frail."

"What's wrong with her?"

"A crippling arthritis. She can't get out of bed."

"You don't help her at all? What do you do for a living?"

"I'm a street vendor."

"You don't sell much and then you drink away the rest."

"How do you know?"

"I can see it in your face. I don't like meeting with guys who have drinking problems."

"I'm your brother."

"That was just an accident of life. We don't choose our brothers. What did you come here for?"

"I want to work so I can send a few pesos to our mother."

"What can you do besides sell junk?"

"I could be your assistant."

Alderete laughed and eyed him with disdain. Rocha began to hate him at that very moment.

"An assistant like you, maybe in a tavern."

"You don't need to make fun of me," Rocha said, half-swallowing his words. "I can do anything."

"Desk work, not a chance. Why don't you start from the bottom? It'll take you awhile to rise, but it's the only way. I'm talking about the deep mine."

"Inside the mine?"

"It's the only way."

Rocha had no choice but to accept. He became a miner, and that's no small matter. Being a miner is like being a sailor on the high seas. If you're the former, you really have to like underground caves, and if you're the latter, it's the ocean. Two unmerciful passions. At first it was very tough. Rocha sometimes thought he was in hell. He rented a room in a pension where it was so cold that even the rats couldn't survive. It was colder inside than outside. He would hang out at miners' dives and once a week go up the hill to a brothel filled with half-breeds. He drank more and more to rid his mind of the underground agony. Becoming a human mole is part of a pact that man makes with the devil. By the end of three months, he had accepted his lot. He got himself a girlfriend who cooked for him and made love to him in sepulchral silence. When he asked her why she didn't moan, she said it was because she didn't want to startle him. Then came the accident, on a Monday, a month before Christmas. They amputated half his leg in the mine hospital. They sawed it off as if he were a soldier in the First World War.

Deciding he was worthless, Alderete gave him a compensation package that was barely enough to bury their mother. Rocha swore that he would get revenge, but the years took him down roads in which there was no time to remember anything, until one day, just about a week earlier, God had granted him a few happy hours in the midst of that bitter existence. It seemed like plenty to him.

He couldn't help himself and took a swig of *pisco*. It made him feel brave.

Despite his limitations, he had managed to read a book: *Treasure Island* by Stevenson. He thought about John Silver, the one-legged pirate, and at times he identified with him. After the rock destroyed part of Rocha's leg, from the knee down, everything had been a pure tragedy for him, with hardly a break to take a breath. A life mapped by a cruel fate, deprived of the slightest relief. Killing Alderete wouldn't be murder; it would be a settling of accounts. He began to sing: *I'm waiting for you, Nazario; Rocha the cripple is going to do you in.* The movements and vibrations of the train felt like the funereal gallop of a black colt, and he, Rocha, was the horseman. With the money that he would collect from this job, he would travel to Iquique, where a black Peruvian woman who had stopped over in La Paz a long time ago was waiting for him. She was a mediocre stage actress, but had been blessed with a pair of shapely thighs molded in Callao. Since the stage didn't yield much dough, she opted to offer her goods in a brothel in that sandy northern Chilean city. She knew about the accident and the stump. *Love doesn't care if you walk like a lame rooster*, she had written him. After all, the damage was only from the knee down; the rest of him was intact and she was happy with the whole package. For the first time in his life, Rocha had something to look forward to. He wouldn't become a millionaire, but there was a room waiting for him on the outskirts of Iquique. He could spend his last days as a doorman there, keeping an eye on the asses of the neighborhood prostitutes. Ending your life on the coast isn't bad; even with an uneasy conscience, time eventually fixes everything. If Alderete wasn't Lucifer's son, he was at least his nephew, and sending him to the eternal fires of hell was a humanitarian act. It would free the country of a snake that leeched off the happiness of others. Rocha thought he should be decorated for what he was about to do.

Suddenly, he heard commotion in the corridor. He picked out the loathsome voice of Alderete. The arrogant tone was still there, even more overbearing than before. Rocha had been advised not to leave his cabin at all, even to go to the bathroom, which is why he had to make do like when he was in the military. The person who hired him had told him that he would get a signal to go out and that he would have a few minutes in which to finish off Alderete. Time was the enemy; Rocha was a cripple on crutches, not an athlete. His hands, however, had acquired the strength that his legs had lost; they were like a pair of pliers, and when he used to choke people during bar fights, the victims would be unable to breathe for several minutes. Rocha studied the damp rag with which he would cut off Alderete's oxygen. He would have to act fast when he got the signal: three knocks on his door. He wasn't a first-class assassin but he was the only one available on the market. Now all he had to do was wait until dark.

Father Moreno was sitting up in bed drinking cinnamon tea. He had lowered the curtain and was dabbing his face with a damp cloth.

"I closed the curtain because of all the dust."

"Good idea," said Ricardo.

"At this altitude, what I eat doesn't go down well. Cinnamon tea helps my digestion. You're young, I imagine you don't have this problem. Youth takes care of everything. Is this your first trip to the coast?"

"My parents have brought me every summer since I was seven years old."

"You're lucky. I've never seen the ocean."

"It's an unforgettable experience."

"Better late than never."

Ricardo washed his face, then dried it with a towel which he'd placed next to the sink and climbed up to his bunk. He closed the curtain, turned on the light above him, and set about to read a chapter of Stendhal's *The Red and the Black*. The brisk swaying of the train and the heat of the cabin put him quickly to sleep. He was awakened by the murmur of a conversation.

"Are you crazy?" exclaimed Father Moreno. "That boy is on the top bunk!"

"So what? He's probably taking a siesta."

"I didn't tell you to come!"

"I wanted to see you. In second class the heat is unbearable. Besides, I can't stand all the crying babies."

"I'm a Franciscan, Carla Marlene! Have you forgotten that?"

Carla Marlene couldn't contain her laughter.

"What are you laughing at?"

"Sorry, I forgot."

"Quiet, he might wake up!" Father Moreno rasped.

Carla Marlene ascended a couple of rungs on the ladder to the upper bunk. She raised the curtain slightly, but Ricardo pretended to be sleeping. She descended cautiously.

"There's nothing like a little nap on a train," she said.

Ricardo held back for several moments and then, with great care, raised the curtain that covered his bunk. To his surprise, he saw Carla Marlene lifting the Franciscan's robe. She unbuckled his belt and pulled down his pants. Father Moreno lay back and closed his eyes. Carla Marlene slipped her head underneath his robe and her hands started to rub the Franciscan's calves. Ricardo could hear the contortionist whispering but couldn't make out the words.

Fantastic! She's giving him a blowjob! he thought.

Carla Marlene, partially covered by the robe, looked like a puppeteer at work. Ricardo was able to glimpse her legs and elbows, which stuck out like the claws of a crab trying to comb through a mound of sand. With the passing minutes, Moreno entered into ecstasy, and the mattress started to shake. He opened his eyes and his dilated pupils appeared to be gazing at heaven; he breathed heavily while grinding his teeth. He was transformed into an erotic chipmunk, while Carla Marlene stamped her feet like an aggrieved old maid.

A minute later, Father Moreno stood up as if he had received an electric shock. Carla Marlene exited the robe with the satisfaction of having done her duty.

"It's hot as hell in here!" she said.

"He didn't wake up?"

"Don't worry. If he wakes up, he'll think that I've had confession and am ready for Holy Communion."

"Don't be blasphemous!"

"Will you take care of my doggy tonight?"

Father Moreno pulled on his pants. "Don't even think of me going with you to the freight car. It's not right for me to be seen with you. The inspector will suspect there's something odd about my concern for that dog."

"Once we've crossed the border, will you take off your habit?"

"Not so loud!"

"Nobody on the train suspects anything."

"How do you know?"

"I just know."

Ricardo, who had calmly witnessed this scene of medieval fellatio, hadn't been mistaken in his suspicions about the priest fellow. From the beginning he seemed like no ordinary cleric. It wasn't only his resemblance to a retired wrestler; it was the way he talked. His speech wasn't resigned like that of the impoverished followers of Saint Francis. *Who is this Moreno guy?* Carla Marlene had sucked him off in a position that looked very uncomfortable. It was no problem for her; since she was a contortionist, she could probably have done it upside down, with the little dog resting under the soles of her feet.

"Don't let them see you leave."

"They'll think I was messing around with the boy." Carla Marlene unlatched the door and leaned out cautiously. "Bye bye," she said, and disappeared.

Father Moreno lay back down. She had left him happy. He softly whistled a Cuban bolero and gradually fell asleep. His expression was beatific. His nap was well-earned.

Ricardo, for a moment, thought he might confess to him that he had seen everything, but Moreno had dressed up as a Franciscan for a reason, and uncovering this now was not advisable.

He decided to go along with the farce. It both amused and intrigued him.

Giulietta found her unfortunate husband still in bed, resting against a pair of pillows. He was doing his accounts in a leather-bound ledger. When he saw her come in, he asked her to sit next to him.

"There's no doctor on the train. Maybe in Charaña we can find a cardiologist."

"Nothing's wrong with my heart. I'm healthier than that pimp Tréllez. You were too young to understand what was happening. When he was ambassador in Paris, that wannabe Frenchman brought back a French girl, one of those department store salesgirls, without his wife knowing it. Of course, he paid for her trip across the ocean and rented her an apartment at the bottom of Seis de Agosto, near the gas station. The jerk visited her every day. The money came from his wife, who owns haciendas on the Altiplano and in the Yungas. He took money from his wife and gave it to the French girl."

"And why did you care?"

"I didn't care."

"So why did you tell her?"

"You believe that nonsense?"

"He told it to your face."

"That moron is a liar."

"He said the French girl didn't pay any attention to you, and that you ratted on him to get revenge."

Alderete tossed the ledger aside, removed his reading glasses, and barked, "You're my wife, right?"

"What does that have to do with it?"

"You can't take that pimp's side. You should believe *me*."

"All right, I believe you," said Gulietta, sounding fatigued. She stood up and fixed her hair in front of the mirror.

"Imagine how pissed those useless society boys must be: a beautiful girl like you, married to me. They can't swallow it."

"Mind if I smoke?" Gulietta asked.

"Of course not. You can do whatever you want. You have married a man who can never say no to you."

Gulietta eyed him as if he were a piece of furniture. "You're looking better. You were very pale."

"Sit here," Alderete ordered.

Gulietta didn't have any choice. Alderete's hands went up her arm until they arrived at her neck. They stopped there and awaited a response. Gulietta remained motionless. Alderete's fingers felt rough and shaky to her.

"I want you so badly," he said.

"We'll be going up to near 16,000 feet," Gulietta remarked.

"So?"

Gulietta smiled. It took great effort for her to treat him with affection. Her feeling of repulsion was stronger than her will. "So, you shouldn't get too aroused at that altitude."

"That's my problem . . . Now turn this way." He took off her sweater and rested a cheek against one of her well-rounded breasts. "Unbutton your bra," he said imperiously.

Gulietta obeyed. She was naked from the waist up. Alderete's nostrils gave off steam like an angry buffalo.

"Your skin is incredible!" he stammered. His lips opened up to receive a drop of youth.

Gulietta could not take her eyes off his greasy mane. She felt one of her nipples being suctioned as if by a rubber doll, and wanted to laugh. Alderete went from one nipple to the other with the expression of a dying man. He continued back and forth for a few minutes, while Gulietta closed her eyes.

"Your skirt," Alderete said. "Take it off."

"It's almost tea time."

"The hell with tea! Do what I say," Alderete grunted.

Gulietta removed him from her naked bust. "After dinner, I'll do whatever you say. Besides, my mother will be here any minute."

"It was stupid of me to bring her on this trip," Alderete said. "I don't know how the old hag convinced me."

"What old hag?"

"Sorry, I didn't mean to offend you."

Gulietta said nothing and put her sweater back on.

"Are you mad at me?"

"My mother is not an old hag. She's a mature lady. Nobody forced you to bring her."

"Yes, she forced me! She said it was part of the deal."

"Deal?"

"Well, part of my promise. She wants to see the United States."

"She protects me. Don't forget that I just graduated from high school. I'm eighteen years old. I've never been with a man before, much less a man who's more than fifty years old. You're old enough to be my father."

"But I'm not. I'm at an enviable age. Experienced but still potent."

Gulietta needed to use the bathroom; she was going to retch. She covered her mouth and left. She crossed the corridor, entered the bathroom, and vomited.

Alderete thought that the girl would stop being difficult once she was on the boat. *She's afraid and she's proud, just like her old man, may he rest in peace. Some of her gestures remind me of the Italian. They don't look alike, but there's an unmistakable family resemblance. The old man used to treat me that way, yet he came to regret it. He had a complex around me. He knew deep down that I was capable of more. It's a shame that he shacked up with that half-breed woman Tomasa; she was sluttier than a hen. This little society girl wants to do the same thing with me, but I'm sharper than her father was. That whole thing about virginity, I believe it and I don't believe it. In Buenos Aires, the gauchos don't put up with that stuff. I know all about that business of the lemon juice and howling with pain. The sister-in-law of that stupid Irishman who got on the train in El Alto tried to tell me that I was the only one. The only sucker.*

Alderete gingerly walked up to the mirror. There wasn't a lot of light, just enough to see himself. Without pleasure, he peered at that face sculpted in mud, half-finished. The sculptor had forgotten to put it in the oven and the model remained formless. It looked like the slightest blow would leave a lifelong dent. His forehead, which was sunken, consumed half his face. His flaccid jowls sagged like those of a bulldog. His jaw was small, without personality. Behind Alderete's reading glasses, his intense eyes were perhaps the only feature worthy of note. His stiff, greasy hair could be mistaken for a fistful of damp hay.

What the hell does that little girl want? If she's not happy, I'm going to make her shape up, whatever the cost. I should never have brought her mother. She's like her mirror. The old lady hates me and tries to hide it. One month in the U.S. and I'll send her back. Nobody rains on my parade. If only my father could see me now—at the pinnacle, damn it. I don't know a word of English, but when you're carrying lots of dollars, they translate for you immediately. I'll buy Gulietta clothes; the cost won't matter. And when I buy them for her, I'll order her not to wear panties in the apartment. That turns me on. I'll make her love me, otherwise I won't have peace.

Gulietta returned from the bathroom. She washed her face and, without a word, went back out.

Alderete found her in the corridor contemplating the landscape, which was signaling the approach of nightfall.

"What's wrong?"

"Nothing."

"Come into the cabin. It's cold out here."

"I want to be alone for a moment."

"I'm sorry for that bit about the old hag. I won't say that again."

Gulietta didn't answer. The steward was sitting at the end of the corridor chewing coca. The train was moving slowly.

"Do you know where we are?" Alderete asked the steward.

"Near the Calacoto station."

Gulietta entered her mother's cabin. Alderete smirked, opened the window, and breathed in the pure air of the Andean plateau.

"I'm a little dizzy," he said to the steward.

"Happens to everybody."

"What's at the border?"

"The Chileans have a barracks."

"How many years have you been working for the railway?"

"About thirty."

"It's time to retire."

"I'll work just one more year. If the opposition wins, they'll nationalize the trains," the steward said.

"That, and my balls."

Alderete breathed calmly. He didn't need to retire. He had enough money to last him two hundred years. Old age was still remote. Death worried him only in his nightmares.

The dust eventually forced him out of the corridor and he returned to his cabin. Doña Clara had told him to change for dinner. She stressed that he would have to get used to the etiquette.

Now it's half-breed Alderete's turn to have a piece of that blue-blood girl, he said to himself.

In cabin number four, Gulietta paced back and forth in front of her mother, who sat with her arms crossed over her chest, examining her distraught face. Gulietta was pale.

"I can't stand him. When he touches me, I feel like throwing up."

"We agreed that you would put up with him for at least a couple of months," Doña Clara said.

"I made a mistake."

"And what do you plan to do?"

"I don't know."

"It will take a few more weeks for the deeds to the house in Obrajes and the other properties to get signed over to your name. You know how bureaucracy moves in our country. That old man could order his lawyer to annul everything. He knows what he's doing."

"If he knows what he's doing, then why did you make a deal with him?"

"Let a couple weeks go by. He's crazy about you. In France they call that state of mind a mid-life crisis, when an older guy falls for a young girl. It's like an illness. You have to take advantage of it."

Gulietta froze and glared at her mother. Doña Clara returned the look.

"That's easy for you to say," Gulietta snapped. "You're not directly involved."

"We made a pact. The idea was to avenge your father. We have to get the money back that Alderete stole."

"That might take months, or years. I can't even stand him for a single night. You don't know what it's like to put up with a pig like him on top of me."

"Did it happen . . . ?"

"Not yet. I'm as much of a virgin as Joan of Arc."

"But you've been married for two days."

"He passed out drunk after our wedding, and last night I put a sleeping pill in his drink."

"You did?"

"I told you, he disgusts me. Don't you understand?"

Doña Clara stood up and kissed her on the forehead. The girl looked very fragile. Gulietta rested her head on her mother's shoulder.

"Don't cry, we'll think of something. I know: Tell him that sex at this altitude is risky because of his high blood pressure. What do you think?"

"The man acts like a beast. If I tell him that, he might try to do it by force, just to prove me wrong. And anyway, I already said something similar and he didn't care."

"He can't force you."

"He's my husband. He has the right."

"Not with violence. If he wants to force you, call for me, I'm right here next door."

Gulietta ran her fine fingers through her mother's hair. "It would've been better not to do this marriage experiment."

"Oh, really? You'd rather be dirt poor?"

"You only think about yourself. You're being selfish. Don't you realize that?"

"I promise you it won't be for very long. You'll get a divorce as soon as we get what we want."

Gulietta lit a cigarette and walked to the window. A few minutes passed in silence. The sun painted a yellow hue over the Altiplano. As small clouds moved across the sky, they would eventually fade away, leaving trails in their wake. Gulietta watched a herd of llamas fleeing across the countryside, frightened by the sound of the train's horn. A peasant boy melancholically observed the locomotive's passing. He was the only human being in all of that desolate space.

"He's looking bad," said Doña Clara. "He has altitude sickness."

"I don't plan on killing him with multiple orgasms. You can be sure of that."

"But if you keep avoiding him, he'll get furious."

"Let him think what he wants. His breathing makes a rattling sound like it's coming up from deep inside his evil soul."

Doña Clara couldn't contain her laughter and sat down on the bed. "It's all my husband's fault."

Gulietta sighed. The light of dusk brought out the best in her; her dark hair revealed silver highlights. "Why?"

"For getting together with that half-breed woman."

"Come on, Mom. You know it's normal for society gentlemen to have lower-class lovers."

"He had never done it before."

"How do you know?"

"She was the first and the last. I know. My heart tells me so."

Gulietta sat down beside her and caressed her hair once again.

"Anyway, it doesn't matter now. That Ricardo boy—did you know him from before?"

"We saw him in Buenos Aires at the house of that poet, Doña Blanca Colorado."

"What year?"

"I was thirteen."

Doña Clara thought for a moment and said: "I remember his mother. But he looks so irresponsible."

"I like him," said Gulietta. "He just graduated from high school like me."

"He has a mischievous face."

"Ricardo isn't my problem right now. Alderete is."

"I'll bet he thinks I'm a snake for making you marry that demon."

"He didn't say anything."

"Everyone thinks I'm a witch."

"A lot of mothers marry off their daughters for money. It's normal."

"But not to their husband's murderer . . ."

"The important thing is to get divorced as soon as possible. He won't know what hit him."

"He's no idiot. First, he has to put some of his property in your name."

"I'm under his skin. He's obsessed with me."

"You can see that from a mile away."

"I'm scared."

"I was a virgin when I married your father."

"Don't make such awful comparisons."

"Your father was a gentleman. I know."

"How was your honeymoon?"

"Romantic and peaceful."

"Where did you go?" Gulietta asked.

"To the Yura hot springs in Peru."

"Working-class people are smarter. They live together before they get married. They call it the *sirwiñacu*."

"Just like the Swedes. And then people say Bolivia is backwards. Anyway, if it doesn't happen tonight with Alderete, he'll ask for it on the ship," Doña Clara said.

"I'll be an undelivered postcard," the daughter responded.

"You can pretend that you're making love to somebody else."

"Somebody like Clark Gable."

Doña Clara shook her head. She was getting nervous; she couldn't keep her hands still for a single moment. She recalled the bitterness that had led her to sacrifice her daughter, the kind of bitterness that can make you lose your sense of good and bad.

"It's my fault," she said.

"It was your idea and I accepted it."

"Well, at least you recognize that. What I want is for you not to suffer. And the problem is, how will that be possible? It's an almost unsolvable dilemma. Don't lose your cool around him. Don't forget that he has something to lose too. If you leave him, he'll panic. His biggest fear is looking like a fool. For him, getting laughed at is worse than a hundred lashes. If you handle the matter intelligently, your father will thank us from heaven."

"You hate him as much as I do."

"Like Iago and Othello."

"I didn't know that you read Shakespeare."

"I've never read him, but your father used to tell me that there was no greater hatred than that of Iago for Othello."

"Shakespeare himself would have been inspired by this moving tragedy. And if he wrote this story, it would probably end with a crime."

"Good God! That's taking it too far."

"He caused my father to take his own life, which makes him the instigator of a suicide. Iago was the one who conspired, but Othello was the weapon."

Doña Clarita frowned. She didn't have any more arguments for convincing Gulietta to go along with the plan. It was at once like a stupid joke and a tragedy. Her thirst for revenge had gone too far. She would've sacrificed herself if she could have, but Alderete wanted a young girl, not an old woman. She hadn't thought for a minute that her daughter would suffer so much.

"I don't know how to fix this," said Doña Clara.

"If he gives me any trouble, I'll scratch his face."

"Alderete has an inferiority complex. He would never dare to hit you."

"You talk as if we're living a hundred years ago."

"That's just the way it is."

Gulietta smiled. Her mother was set in her ways—she had been raised on notions of class that undergirded a decadent society, one that refused to accept that the country was changing.

"Where is that Alderete?" asked Doña Clara.

"Sleeping, I suppose."

The afternoon was fading as the train came to a halt. The station had a corrugated-metal roof and was surrounded by flowers. It sat alone on the outskirts of a tiny mud and straw village. Next to the station stood a weeping willow with a couple of cats playing around it. In the distance there was a plaza rimmed by eucalyptus trees.

The sun, partially hidden behind the mountains, shone down on a small adobe church. The church's towers dominated the village. A man on a bicycle was circling the plaza. There was also a single store, in the doorway of which stood a woman staring out at the train. The Bolivian Railway inspector stepped down onto the station platform.

Gulietta was in the dining car drinking tea with lemon and smoking when Ricardo arrived. Her gaze abruptly ceased its wandering across the horizon.

"I'll have a coffee," Ricardo told the waiter, then turned to Gulietta "Are you waiting for him?"

"For my prison guard? No way."

"He might hit me."

"He sleeps like a bear."

"How long will you be staying in Arica?"

"One day. At night, we'll board one of the *Santa* ships to New Orleans. I think it's the *Santa Rita.* It's a freighter with luxury cabins."

"It'll be easier for you to put up with him. The comforts will help—the pool, the good food."

"Don't be ridiculous. I don't even want to think about it. I might jump overboard."

"Why don't you just throw *him* overboard?"

"He's too heavy. I'd need help."

"There are always drunken sailors. The Yankees got their love of rum and violence from the Brits."

"Ricardo . . ."

"Yes?"

"Will the Franciscan stay in your cabin?"

"I don't know."

"I . . . Could I go there in a few minutes?"

Ricardo fell silent. His eyes did the talking, then he said out loud, "Don't worry; I've got a good reason for him to take a walk."

Ricardo called the waiter, paid, and headed for his cabin. The Franciscan was reading a newspaper. When he saw Ricardo come in, he produced a Bible from underneath his blanket.

"Father," said Ricardo, "I'd like to be alone in the room for a while."

"Really?"

"Yes, Father."

"And you would like me to go out for a walk on the Altiplano."

"You could go out for a cup of tea."

"Young man, I think you're showing me a lack of respect."

Ricardo moved up to within two hand lengths of his nose. The little priest stood up. He was eight inches shorter, but more than sixty pounds heavier.

"I saw you with Carla Marlene . . ."

Instead of standing taller, the Franciscan shrunk. He recoiled like a servant preparing to haul a cartful of mail.

"What are you saying?"

"Do I need to explain?"

"You mean you spied—"

"I saw everything."

"So you weren't asleep?"

"I get the impression you are not a priest."

Father Moreno smiled. "Have you seen me before?"

"No."

"I'm a leader of mine workers."

"And why are you disguised?"

Father Moreno invited him to sit down. From a knapsack, he removed a clipping from the newspaper *Última Hora*. Ricardo slowly read the article explaining the lead role of a fellow named Ignacio Torres in hunger strikes, protest marches, and other rebellious acts in the Catavi and Siglo XX mines. Ricardo recognized Father Moreno in the photo in the center of the article; he had long hair and wore a *lluchu* hat. He had a beard, and a mustache like that of a Mexican rancher.

"Are you on the run?"

"You don't need to be too smart to reach that conclusion. The mine bosses' political police have my number. If they catch me they'll take me straight to jail. I have to make it to Chile. I'll live in self-exile until things change. You don't know much about politics, do you?"

"I don't, unfortunately. I don't like politics."

"Whether or not you like it isn't the point. It's part of your life. In Bolivia, anyone who stays out of politics is despicable."

"If you say so."

"Well . . . things can't go on like this. Or do you think we're in the best of worlds?"

"I don't know."

"Later, when there's time, I'll tell you about the Bolivian left. But first you have to promise me that, to you, I am still Father Moreno. Otherwise, I'll consider you an informant. Not a word, please."

"You don't need to get all worked up, Father. I'll still think of you as a poor friar, a follower of Saint Francis."

"That's more like it. You and I will make a good team. I'll go to the dining car and have a cup of tea. Could you loan me ten pesos?"

Father Moreno stopped for a moment in the corridor and took in the natural environment outside. The sun now hid discreetly behind the mountains, caressing them, bidding farewell to the wild landscape.

As the sun receded further, it gave way to shadows announcing the hostile Altiplano night, accompanied by an anguished silence.

Ricardo paced nervously from one side of the cabin to the other. He turned on the light. The heat wasn't on yet and the temperature in the cabin was still pleasant. Fifteen minutes passed and Gulietta still hadn't shown up. Ricardo went from nervous hopefulness to disappointment.

He wondered about the true motive behind Gulietta's proposal. It wasn't to bother him with more about her husband; she could have done that in the dining car. The way she carried on had thrown Ricardo off. He realized perfectly well that he was going to be used. He was a kind of counterweight to Gulietta's emotional imbalance, providing potential relief for her sorrow. He didn't know her very well, but from their few conversations on the train, he concluded that she was going through tough times. Marrying a guy she hated, who'd had a lot to do with her father's death, had clearly been a mistake that was affecting her deeply. But what was done was done. Getting used wasn't a big deal. However, he had never found himself in this kind of situation with a girl who was his social equal. All things considered, he liked Gulietta and was willing to indulge her whims without worrying about the consequences.

Finally she arrived. She entered the cabin and took a deep breath.

"Nobody saw you?"

"The steward gave me a funny look. This must happen all the time on trains."

The locomotive accelerated its pace. The cars appeared to be dancing between the sides of the rails. The train swerved and Gulietta ended up in Ricardo's arms. She didn't move. Ricardo held her and kissed her on the lips. When he placed his hands on her breasts, she let out a sigh of pleasure.

"My husband and I, we haven't even come close."

"Is he impotent?"

"Not really."

"Then you didn't want to."

"Let's just say that a mysterious force kept the marriage from being consummated."

"And tonight? On trains it's impossible to resist temptation. Alderete won't forgive you."

"You talk as if I were the slave of an Ottoman chief."

"What can you do to resist him?"

"I don't know."

She lay down to rest on the bed and Ricardo curled up at her side.

"You're trembling," he said.

"Do you think I do this every day?"

She unbuttoned her blouse and removed her bra; her breasts were quivering. She closed her eyes and took Ricardo's hand between hers. He caressed her hesitant adolescent body like a starfish maneuvering around submerged rocks.

"I'm really scared the priest will show up," said Gulietta.

At that moment, Ricardo was overcome by an uncontrollable passion, but it intimidated her and she stopped him cold. "Are you a virgin too?" she asked.

"What?"

"Take it easy."

"Aren't you turned on?"

"Yes, but I could use some more caressing."

Ricardo tried to steady himself. He closed the curtain and saw that she was trembling, then they joined together in a long embrace. He could feel her heart pounding; her lips opened and closed nervously.

Without separating himself from her tremulous skin, Ricardo scooted down until he reached the top buttons of her skirt. With one hand he unbuttoned her skirt; with the other he scaled her warm thighs. The moment they felt his touch, they squeezed together, concealing her sex, a shadow covered by silk panties.

But then she raised her bottom, allowing Ricardo to remove the panties. The veering of the train was now accompanied by the sound of grinding metal, making it hard for him to concentrate.

"Has anybody seen my wife?"

It was the hoarse and congested voice of Alderete out in the corridor, presumably addressing the steward.

"Now of all times," said Ricardo.

Gulietta pulled herself up, leaning against the head of the bed.

"He can't give me a moment of peace," she said, starting to whimper.

"We can still do it," said Ricardo, who felt that one of the best asses he had ever seen was slipping between his fingers.

"I can't. I'll go back to my cabin. We'll have to wait. We still have time."

"Forget about him."

"It's not that. I'm just not into it right now."

"I'm into it enough for the both of us."

"I'm sorry, Ricardo."

"Will you go back on your promise?"

"Later. I swear."

She slipped her panties back on and dried her tears. Smiling benevolently, she ran her fingers timidly through Ricardo's hair. He couldn't believe his bad luck.

Alderete's presence in the corridor had ruined their erotic prelude. Gulietta's amorous disposition had been replaced by a contained fury; hearing her husband's voice had brought her back to a reality she had hoped to escape from for at least half an hour. Alderete kept them hanging a few minutes, until he eventually decided to return to his cabin.

Gulietta stepped out into the corridor. The steward observed her sympathetically. Through the window, the landscape reinvented itself from moment to moment; it was like watching an endless movie, one without pauses or surprises. The Altiplano was a horizontal vertigo, as Drieu de la Rochelle once wrote about the Argentine pampas. Human life had vanished, giving way to a desolate moonscape. Gulietta contemplated the anguished scenery with a kind of juvenile sadness.

On his way back from the dining car, Father Moreno found the girl lost in thought, arms crossed and leaning against the windowsill. He didn't bother to interrupt her reverie, he simply knocked on his cabin door. Ricardo came out into the corridor.

"A penny for his thoughts," said Gulietta in English when Moreno headed into the cabin.

"A half an hour; not a minute less, not a minute more," said Ricardo.

Gulietta couldn't keep from laughing.

"These priests have a sixth sense," said Gulietta. "I bet you he thinks I'm scandalous; just married and spotted in someone else's cabin."

"He's going to start praying for your soul," said Ricardo.

"Let's hope he gets an answer to his prayers and then tells me what it is."

Alderete's generous silhouette suddenly appeared. He had a hard time concealing his emotions; he was nearly tongue-tied. "Are you going to the cabin?" he managed to stutter.

Gulietta brushed Ricardo's hand, signaling both goodbye and see-you-soon. She marched off, but instead of moving to her own cabin, she entered her mother's.

"Were you in the same class?" Alderete asked Ricardo.

"We both graduated from high school last year."

"A very young woman with an older man. It must seem strange to you."

"On the BBC from London I heard that an eighty-year-old guy married a twenty-two-year-old girl. They're crazy about each other."

Alderete smiled flatly. His face had the impassivity of the Tiwanaku statues.

"Love is mainly spiritual," said Ricardo. "What really matters in marriage is friendship, personal compatibility."

Alderete tried to discern sarcasm in Ricardo's words, to no avail.

"What do eighteen-year-olds talk about?"

"I don't know . . . Bogart movies and Platters records."

"Have you been to the United States?"

"No."

"We're going there. We'll be disembarking in New Orleans and from there to New York."

"You're a lucky man. And I hear you're rich."

"That's life for you."

A moment later, Ruiz emerged from the dining car. He was wearing a frayed orange coat. "A cold night is upon us," he said. "How's it going, Don Nazario?"

Alderete did not acknowledge the greeting. He had a way of ignoring people who were of no use to him, whether in business or in his social aspirations.

"Hi," said Ricardo.

"Don Nazario, I'm here to invite you to an after-dinner card game," said Ruiz.

"Don't you know yet that it's nearly impossible to beat me at cards?"

"We'll take our chances."

"Who's playing?"

"The Marquis, Petko, Durbin, and me."

"And that Tréllez guy?"

"He doesn't play poker, he plays bridge."

"Like all faggots."

"He's not a faggot; womanizer would be more like it."

"Invite him. If he goes, I'll go," said Alderete.

"Got it," said Ruiz.

"I'll put in a bottle of whiskey, you guys put in another one. What do you say?"

"I'll ask."

"Don't be so tight."

"Fine." Ruiz looked at him with a rancor that was difficult to hide.

Alderete was enjoying the moment. "You better not fix the cards."

"You've got to be kidding, Don Nazario."

"I'll whip you all," Alderete said, then turned to Ricardo. "You don't play?"

"I play badly."

"Ricardo's a good kid. We have to keep him away from cards," said Ruiz.

Alderete smirked at Ruiz. "I've never seen a coat this color before."

"I bought it from a Jewish friend of mine."

"I can tell." Alderete eyed Ruiz as he walked off.

"I won some land from him near the Soligno factory once. I screwed him over because he was out of line."

"And nobody's screwed you over before?"

"I'm a born winner."

"There's nothing wrong with losing every now and then."

Alderete looked the young man over from head to toe. "You're a loser. I can see it in your face."

"You don't know me."

"You're an unlucky beginner."

"Not in everything. Sometimes things go well for me. I'm lucky with women."

"Gulietta's little ass is mine. Try imagining you're with her when you jerk off tonight."

"Don't make me disrespect you."

"You've been circling around her since the train left. Gulietta is my wife. Tomorrow we're taking one of the *Santa* ships and that'll be it."

"You're a sick man. You need a psychiatrist."

"Sick or not, she's my wife."

"Nobody denies that."

"What do you want then?"

"Nothing. She's just a friend."

"You won't see her for many years, maybe never again. An adventure on a train with a married woman—is that what's missing from your repertoire?"

"You've got quite an imagination, even though you're only an accountant."

"If you keep bothering her, then I'll have to use my fists."

"Why don't we get off at the next station? That way we can see what you can do with those fists."

"Careful, pretty boy."

"Better a pretty boy than someone who kisses pretty boys' asses."

Alderete took a step forward. Ricardo stepped back, removed his jacket, and handed it to the steward, who was observing the drama unfold as if he were sitting in an armchair watching a magic show.

"I won't hit you because Gulietta would make a scene."

"See? I'm a lucky kid."

"Laugh all you want, but tonight I'll have her in my bed."

Ricardo asked Alderete to move aside so he could get to the dining car. Alderete, in spite of himself, complied.

One of the waiters appeared right then, ringing a small bell and knocking on the cabin doors. "Time to sign up for dinner," he called out.

Father Moreno stuck his impertinent stevedore's face out of his cabin door. Alderete frowned and the Franciscan vanished immediately.

"That little priest, I know him from somewhere. What's his last name?" Alderete asked the waiter.

The man flipped through a notebook. "Moreno. Daniel Moreno. He's a Franciscan."

"I'm not very religious, but I'm sure I've seen that bastard before."

"He's a Franciscan."

"You already told me that. Do you think I'm deaf?" Alderete slowly retraced his steps, trying to remember where he could have seen that face.

Looking at her reflection in the mirror, Anita asked her cabin mate: "Do you think my outfit is too loud?"

Gulietta was smoking and she could still feel Ricardo's caresses on her body.

"Some people don't like red," said Doña Clara.

"I've got a white one that I use when I go to the Tabarís with the girls."

"What girls?"

"The nightclub hostesses . . ."

Doña Clara had never heard that term before. She went to the window. On the horizon, a ray of sunlight broke the opacity of twilight. She looked out on a row of mountains illuminated by the intense light.

"You must have an interesting life," said Doña Clara.

"Ha!"

"What did you use to work in?" asked Gulietta.

"Nothing but nightclubs, ever since I was seventeen years old in Valparaíso. At twenty-five I came to Bolivia. Life is very hard over there in Chile. I retired just two years ago. You know, darling, for certain things, gentlemen prefer youth. Since I retired I've been managing several houses and recruiting girls for friends like the Marquis. I only work with serious people."

Doña Clara stood there with her eyes wide open, not even blinking. "Of course . . ."

"I've known the Marquis since I managed my first house in Caiconi, over there above Miraflores. I also met his wife. Once in Valparaíso, she invited me to her restaurant, which was popular with the chic crowd. Your husband . . ."

"Continue," said Gulietta. "What happened with my husband?"

Anita blushed, something that didn't occur very often.

"Go on, Anita," said Doña Clara.

"Nazario stole his wife."

"Marquis's?"

"You didn't know?"

"No," said Gulietta. "How did it happen?"

"They were friends and Alderete was going through tough times. The Marquis let him live at his house out of the goodness of his heart. One day he came back early from soccer and found them in bed together. He wanted to kill him."

"And why didn't he?"

"The thing is, Gulietta, the Marquis is a sentimental guy. Besides, his old lady started crying. The little bitch got the house and they split the restaurant. If your husband's not a saint, please don't be upset with me."

"He's a bastard," replied Gulietta.

"Don't swear," snipped Doña Clara.

"Poor Marquis," said Gulietta. "So he hates him."

"He doesn't even want to see his face."

Anita changed her outfit. She was a strong woman who exhibited a certain voluptuousness, though her white skin reflected the stress of hundreds of carnal encounters. Even so, her character was that of a high-society woman and it took a great deal of perceptiveness to divine her past. Over time, she had lost most of her Chilean accent, but traces of it remained. She was attentive, respectful, and a trustworthy friend.

Her career as a hooker, and subsequently a madam, didn't stop her from being a sensible matron who adhered to certain rules of the game with respect to Bolivia's prevailing Victorian morality.

"I need air," said Anita. "I'd rather fly a thousand times, even though it scares me to fly. How can you stand him, Gulietta?"

"I can't stand him. When he touches me, my hair stands on end."

"That's really something, since his skin is smooth like a Chihuahua."

Doña Clara couldn't keep from laughing. Gulietta coughed and then let out a guffaw that could be heard as far as the dining car.

"And you, Anita, how did you put up with them?"

"I stayed focused on the money that came in."

"You were so brave!" said Doña Clara.

"It just takes time. Once I went to bed with a sailor they used to call Baby Seal. He didn't have legs or arms, just a torso. I picked him up and put him on top of me as if he were a doll and gave him the orgasm of his life."

Gulietta and her mother collapsed into each other's arms laughing.

"Take it easy, my darling," Doña Clara said. "You won't get anywhere by stirring up trouble."

"Give him a tranquilizer tonight," suggested Anita.

"I already gave him one yesterday."

"Then there's no way around it."

"No, there isn't, but he won't get a virgin."

"What? And who . . . ?" asked Doña Clara.

"I've already planned it out."

Doña Clara grabbed her by the shoulders. "Don't even think of it."

"It's up to me," said Gulietta. "Leave this to me at least."

"Ricardo?" asked her mother.

"It's my revenge. My very personal revenge."

Anita took a small mirror out of her purse and put on lipstick. Mother and daughter looked on in silence.

"Personal?"

"You'll see."

"Don't do anything stupid that you'll regret later. Alderete will make you pay."

"And he's my father's murderer. Or did you forget?"

"I'll never forget."

"So?"

The train left the Altiplano and began climbing up a steep mountain pass. The locomotive, huffing and puffing, advanced laboriously. The engineer wiped his face, which was streaked with soot. One of the coal men handed him a shot of *pisco*. Even though Quispe traversed this section a couple of times a week, each time felt just as exhilarating as the first.

"When do you think we'll be arriving in Charaña?" asked the coal worker.

"Midnight, as long as the engine doesn't break down," said Quispe.

Night continued to fall as the train climbed toward the summit. The sun looked like a reddish moon on the horizon as the engine's churning echoed over the mountain.

"You say I play with that bastard?" Petko asked.

Ruiz combed back a clump of black hair sticking out over his forehead like an Apache warrior.

"He says he's going to whip us all," said Ruiz.

"I not used to play with strangers and tricksters, but if he wants to play with Petko, I have no problem."

"Let's not make him think we're afraid of him," said Durbin.

The Irishman had been an employee of the Bolivian Railway for ten years and, after a period as a chief inspector, had retired with an excellent pension that paid him in British pounds. He was a big man, of the size and build one would expect to find in Canada guarding forests and hunting wolves. It was strange for an Irishman of pure stock to wind up in an English company, but his first father-in-law had been a Londoner and it was he who helped Durbin get the job. Durbin's English wife died of tuberculosis, so to help get his mind off his loss, he asked the company he was working with in Liverpool for an exotic assignment. They sent him to the Bolivian Railway, which was like posting him to Katmandu. He anchored his tormented soul in Uyuni, a major railway center with connections to Argentina and Chile. At first he suffered from the high altitude and the cold, but later he met Lourdes, a teacher overcome by solitude and seemingly destined for permanent spinsterhood. Lourdes wasn't pretty, but it was her luck that she fit the bill for Durbin. She was thin and pale, with dark eyes like those of a girl from India. He was the second man she had ever been with. The first was a medical student who emigrated to Brazil, and who, according to news reports, had been cut to pieces at a farm in Matto Grosso. She adopted the Irishman as if he was her own child. He gave her economic stability and she brought him that feminine touch which was missing from his disorderly existence; he drank like a Cossack, frequented sordid brothels, and fought every day with the Bolivian Railway employees, whom he considered lazy and irresponsible. His life slowly became organized. He stopped seeing whores, and even though Lourdes was no Marilyn Monroe, she put a lid on his sexual incontinence. An Irishman built like him needed an ardent woman, but she forced him to move at her pace: a traditional, academic-style sexual schedule: once at night and once in the morning. She wasn't sensual, but she didn't like her students to teach her class. In bed, she was both an educator and a wench. He slowly got used to freezing cold Uyuni. He continued drinking beer but moderated his Celtic violent streak. She took him to the movies every day and he became a dedicated film buff. He loved romantic movies and crime flicks in which black men and other people of color who resembled his fellow moviegoers had the daylights beaten out of them. They were childless and she assured him it was because of the altitude and the climate, even though Durbin never ceased to be amazed at how the miners, despite the squalor in which they lived, managed to have five kids per capita.

He knew the ex-accountant, Alderete. Lourdes's sister, a girl named Inés, had been the man's lover for a good while in Potosí, where she lived with her parents. Back then, Alderete was Carletti's accountant in the Encantada mine. The girl had gotten pregnant, which didn't please her family or Alderete, who saw in his future descendant an obstacle to his career as an ambitious bureaucrat. Inés, who was young, naïve, and gullible, gave in to Nazario's repeated urgings and had an abortion at the hands of a half-breed midwife in Oruro. Sadly, Inés did not survive. Lourdes had secretly sworn to kill Alderete without her husband's knowledge, yet after a while she dropped the idea and forgot her promise to herself. But when she saw him on the train, she remembered her sister and blood rushed to her face. Just being near him was enough to make her shudder.

"He made fun of my orange coat," said Ruiz with the face of a hurt child.

"Is your fault, what you approach this bastard for? *Khuya*[*]. Do not think that bastards change with time. They stay that way until death," said Petko.

"He doesn't like Jews," said Ruiz, jabbing at Petko.

"I do not give shit what he says," said Petko. "Tonight I sharpen my fingers to take all money he has."

"Will you talk to Moses?" asked the Marquis.

"Moses lawmaker, Jehovah God. Do not be so ignorant, Marquis. You spent too much time at Tabarís. Too many women mess up your head."

Tréllez preened in front of the mirror like a Rio de Janeiro dandy from the '40s. His face was certainly special; it looked like a Venetian carnival mask crafted by a madman.

"I assume you'll be staying at the Hotel Pacífico, Petko?"

"Where else I stay? Other hotels are for low-class people."

"I'm not low class," the Marquis snapped. "But I'm staying at the Madrid."

"Your case different. You have hostesses over; you cannot stay at Hotel Pacífico. They do not let you in," said Petko.

"It bothers you that I get to hook up with pretty Chilean girls, while you're stuck with yourself," replied the Marquis.

"I go to rest and meditate," said Petko.

"And think about all the money you're putting away," added Ruiz.

[*]*Russian expletive.*

"Petko put away money? I spend everything. My apartment at EMUSA building costs a ton, and then the suits, and nights out with friends . . ."

"Good thing that half-breed chick doesn't cost you anything," said Durbin.

"I not drunk Irishman," said Petko. "I not raise hell in Uyuni bars beating up half-breeds."

Durbin started laughing, and the others followed suit.

Petko lit a cigar. "Each one costs nearly a dollar," he said. "Straight from Cuba."

"What are you going to do with all this money you're saving? Or can you use it in Jewish heaven?" asked Ruiz with a mischievous smile.

"Our heaven different. Abstract. No sexless little angels playing harps."

Petko stood about 5'4". He had lived in Gorki during the difficult Stalinist period, when dear father Joseph started to eliminate intellectuals and Jewish bankers, accusing them of imperialist plots. He fled in trucks, concealed under sacks of potatoes, and on foot, through inhospitable land where any citizen could be a spy helping the local authorities with their witch hunts. After a few months, frozen and hungry, he arrived at the Hungarian border. From there he traveled to France, where a Jewish organization that assisted refugees helped him ship out to South America. He arrived in Bolivia with a few Argentine pesos in his pocket, but before long he became economically stable, and within a year had evolved into a kind of banker for the Jewish community. He was intelligent and wise, not very cultured but possessing an extraordinary business sense. He was a regular at the Club de La Paz café and knew everybody. He was a hardened misogynist, but also outgoing and loquacious. Some people thought he was a nice guy; others considered him impertinent. He was on his way to Arica to pick up imported goods for a textile factory owned by one of his compatriots. Sometimes he would act as intermediary and charge a commission in dollars. Seizing the moment, Petko would stay in Arica for a few days taking in the sun and try to bring his elevated red blood cell count—common among people living in La Paz—down to a reasonable level.

"Durbin talk about half-breed woman. I have half-breed woman and guarantee you is most exquisite thing. I cannot compare with Tabarís girls or rich girls with fur coats, but guarantee you that this half-breed girl makes me happy. She tastes like the earth. She know everything naturally and do not have to take classes in Marquis apartment."

"I met your French girl," Marquis said to Tréllez. "She was a real babe."

"Alderete made her go back to France. He offered to buy her an apartment, but that son of Satan couldn't please her even with a million dollars."

"I used to see her walking an enormous dog at the Plaza Avaroa," remarked the Marquis.

"I bought it from Carlos Víctor Aramayo, the tin baron," said Tréllez. "He sold it to me because it used to eat the plants at his house on Avenida Arce . . . She was a delicious girl," he continued nostalgically. "I met her in Paris in the Lafayette department store. She was a saleswoman. Back then I was Bolivia's ambassador."

"You couldn't resist," said Durbin.

"An ambassador is an ambassador, despite the fact that our country isn't exactly a superpower. I miss her, even though it's been a few years since I last saw her."

"Devil sent that Alderete bastard to earth to do evil bidding. Everything I hear about him involves dirty trick."

"Did he do anything to you?" asked the Marquis.

"We do not run in same circles," said Petko. "He lives in mining towns."

"They tell me he could be named a minister in Ballivián's next cabinet."

"It wouldn't surprise me," said the Marquis. "He has an impressive résumé."

"Marquis," said Petko, "you an MNR man. Your future is set."

"They've been giving us a hard time lately. I'm just a businessman, a little sui generis, but a businessman in the end."

"Girls to you like product: use and replace."

"Don't be so blunt," Ruiz said.

"The Marquis is like a father to these girls. Better that they fall into his hands than into the clutches of another," Durbin asserted with a tone of benevolence.

"You should marry. Go from one girl to other, bad for your spirit. Lascivious."

"Hey, we should be planning how to attack Alderete tonight," suggested Ruiz.

"Want pull fast one?"

"It wouldn't be a bad idea," said the Marquis.

"I not need tricks to bust that bastard," said Petko.

"He stole my wife, which is worse than losing property," said the Marquis.

"I used to think about building a house for my children. Now I rent a place. I was never able to buy myself another one," said Ruiz.

"You're not old," said Durbin. "You'll have another chance. There are thousands of properties, but not stolen wives. The Marquis has a dagger in his heart."

"Property is bullshit," said Petko. "Stir up trouble for piece of land not right for adult man. I not help with tricks, but sometimes I can wink an eye."

"Thanks," replied Ruiz. "Now I need a drink."

"Let's have whiskey," said Tréllez. "Only a fine drink at this time of day."

"Don't think anymore about that guy," advised Durbin.

"That poor girl," said Petko. "Of course, women cannot be messed with. Man think with logic and they pure instinct. Instinct is stronger than logic. Prehistoric animals like tortoises are still alive, after millions of years. Not with logic, but following instinct. Man will not last millions of years on earth."

"The Martians are coming," said Ruiz.

"Martians are only in Hollywood. We will screw everything up without help of extraterrestrials," said Petko.

"For special occasions, I keep a deck of marked cards," said Ruiz.

"Alderete is no pushover," Durbin responded. "Marked cards are child's play."

"I not play with marked cards," said Petko.

"It's okay," concluded Ruiz. "There will be another way."

The train descended once again toward the plateau. As it braked, a sharp screeching noise arose from the engine rings. The train passed through a long, rocky tunnel and emerged like a caterpillar desperate for fresh air.

"So he took away your property," said the Marquis.

Ruiz lowered his eyes. He tried to avert the other man's gaze, but then the images of that night returned, confusing but sharp. He could see the figure of Alderete in front of him at a gigantic table. The ex-accountant looked like a toad about to devour him. He was laughing and flashing a fan-shaped mass of cards that made Ruiz dizzy.

"What are you thinking about?" asked Durbin.

"Revenge," said Ruiz.

"*Vengeance is mine; I will repay, saith the Lord.* Even the Bible talks about it; it's not a bad thing. If it's just, it's a moral act. If he wronged you, you can wrong him back."

"I'll need help," said Ruiz.

"We'll be there," confirmed Tréllez. "If you need an ace, we'll pass you one. What do you all say?"

"Leave me out," said Petko. "I screw that half-breed with own weapons."

"Your revenge will be ours," said the Marquis.

"I go for walk in dining car," said Petko.

They had to open a window since Petko had polluted the air with cigar smoke. The cold gusts of the highlands seemed to be punishing that forgotten corner of the earth.

"At the table next to the kitchen, there is a mirror behind the seat," Durbin thought out loud. "If we can get Alderete to sit right there, somebody from the next table over could see his cards and tip us off."

"I think Anita would be willing to volunteer," the Marquis speculated. "There's no love lost between her and that ambitious little accountant."

"The hard part will be getting him to sit there," said Ruiz.

"We'd have to sit down first, wait for him, and then get him seated. Don't let him have a choice," suggested Tréllez.

"He's sharp, he'll notice," the Marquis remarked.

"We'll run the risk," said Durbin. "Just like Petko, I don't like cheating. But I'm still with you guys."

"Don't act like you're above all this," the Marquis responded.

"We've got to get him drunk," said Ruiz. "He loves whiskey. With a few drinks, he'll lose his head."

"He said he'd bring a bottle," the Marquis reminded them.

"As much as he hates me, he'll be in quite a mood," Tréllez said.

"Don't provoke him, Durbin," the Marquis advised.

"I'll have a hard time controlling myself, but I'll pray for my blood to cool."

"If you hit him, everything will go to hell," said Ruiz. "Durbin, you're a hot head."

"I said I'll control myself."

"There's nothing left to do except wait for dinner and prepare the ambush," said Tréllez.

"We better not miss out on that table," added Ruiz. "I'll go reserve it right now."

"Give the waiter a few pesos," said Tréllez.

"We'll split it."

"What a tightwad," said Durbin.

"All right . . . all right . . . no need for insults."

The train plunged into the most arid part of the Altiplano. Night fell definitively over the pampas. Outside, the blackness was startling. An occasional flickering light could be made out, nothing but a candle in a mud hut lost in the darkness.

Alderete changed into another suit for dinner. He was in a good mood despite the verbal exchange with Ricardo. He was a malicious guy, and his emotions came and went like the wind. His only obsession had been money, but now he had a new one: Gulietta. He was married to her, and this calmed him. *Tonight it'll be hard for her to resist. But if she does it will be even better, whimpering and all.*

In the corridor, the three women were waiting for him. Alderete gulped and took Gulietta and Doña Clara aside.

"What are you doing with that Anita? She's a madam. Do you know what that means?"

"She said she used to own a pension for girls in La Paz," said Doña Clara.

"She trafficks in whores from Chile. She places them in brothels and in the Tabarís of that big-nosed Marquis."

"She told us that you made his wife leave him. Is that true?" asked Gulietta.

Alderete's face didn't turn red, but only because his skin never changed its color.

The dining car was bursting with people. When they'd heard that the chef had prepared chicken and pasta, the best dish at that café on wheels, many second-class passengers crowded right in. They filled the car from end to end. The ambience was festive. The travelers' good mood contrasted with the oppressive environment on that steppe, which seemed to be moving ever closer to the sky. The people were talking animatedly and loud guffaws could be heard from the table where Durbin and company were seated. Ricardo, in the midst of the racket, spotted an open seat right in front of the painter from second class. Apparently, nobody dared sit with him. His disheveled Russian *mujik* look would frighten anyone, but Ricardo had no choice but to sit down. Soon after, Gulietta appeared; trailing her were Alderete, Doña Clara, and Anita. His eyes followed her. She looked magnificent.

When Alderete saw that Anita was about to sit down at the table he had reserved, he said: "I see your friend the Marquis over there."

"Anita is our guest," said Gulietta.

Alderete's face took on a deferential expression.

"Where's Ricardo?" asked Doña Clara. "You told me he would dine with us."

Gulietta looked around for him. Ricardo raised his hand.

"I had a few words with him," said Alderete. "He's very interested in my wife."

"What did you tell him?"

"To stop following you around because you're married to me."

Gulietta's face turned red. "I married you, but I'm not your property. I want you to get that idea into your head. I don't belong to anybody."

"I know his family," said Doña Clara. "It's one of the best in La Paz."

Every time Doña Clara alluded to certain people's ancestry, Alderete would nearly have a fit. It was the only thing he hadn't been able to buy yet: a family lineage that would render him immune to slights from the people with whom he wanted to rub elbows. His marriage to Gulietta was his secret hope for cautiously entering the high social circles of La Paz.

"This doesn't give him the right to pester Gulietta," said Alderete.

"Who told you it bothers me?"

"In any case, I saw it coming."

"Your jealousy pisses me off," said Gulietta.

"Now you're talking like a gaucho," replied Alderete. "What do you mean *pisses me off?*"

"That it pisses me off, that it makes me fu—"

"Please, Gulietta," her mother cut in. "Alderete, you have to remember that she's barely eighteen years old."

Gulietta summoned a waiter. A chubby guy with an obsequious smile immediately approached. White jacket, black bow tie, and hair slicked back Carlos Gardel–style, with plenty of pomade. He announced the menu and paused.

"A bottle of Concha y Toro, red," said Alderete.

"White," corrected Gulietta. "If we eat chicken, it'll be white. Red goes with steak."

"The young lady is right," said the waiter.

"The lady," stressed Alderete, "is my wife. I want red wine and I'm having red wine. I couldn't care less if it goes with chicken or with steak."

"Let's leave it at that," said Doña Clara.

The engine whistled. The train was gradually decelerating. Anita used a handkerchief to wipe away the dust that had accumulated on the windowsill. Several shacks covered in thick fog could be seen a few hundred yards in the distance.

The painter pulled back his hair every time he raised his soup spoon to his mouth. His abundant mane was agitated by the slightest puff of wind that penetrated the cracks in the window.

"It's good," he said. "It's corn chowder."

Ricardo saw the contortionist chatting away with a woman wrapped in a black shawl, who listened in prudent silence.

Father Moreno managed to settle in at the edge of one of the tables, next to four women with the unmistakable look of contraband dealers.

"My name is Pastor Iñiga," said the painter. "I only paint seascapes. Have you ever heard of me?"

"I don't know much about the fine arts in our country."

"I'm a protest artist," he said. "I've been everywhere in Latin America. My last show was in Brazil. They'd never seen anything like it."

"How so?"

"In my canvases, the sea is black and the crest of the waves is red. The blood of our patriots."

"Ah!"

"Will you be there for a good while?"

"Fifteen days."

"I can't stand those Chileans," said Iñiga. "I'll stay three days and then head back."

Alderete, meanwhile, was trying to uncork the wine with alarming ineffectiveness.

"I'll open it," said Gulietta. She took the bottle and uncorked it dexterously.

"Why are you looking at me like that?" asked Alderete.

"Like what?"

Doña Clara could sense another row coming on, the kind that recurred several times a day. And that was only the beginning. She noticed that her daughter was making superhuman efforts to control her temper, which at times could be explosive. The girl was suffering; it was obvious. Only when her gaze met Ricardo's was she able to distract herself—with the memory of their cuddling in the cabin.

"Tomorrow we'll be at sea," mused Doña Clara. "They tell me the *Santas* are excellent ships. I understand they only have a few cabins."

"The tickets are extremely expensive," said Alderete.

"Let's enjoy it while we can," said Doña Clara. "Next thing you know, the MNR will take over and we'll be toast."

"That and the face of God I'll never see," said Alderete. "They won't be back."

"Have they been there before?" asked Anita.

"Paz was Villaroel's finance minister."

"Good grief, the politics in this country!" exclaimed Anita.

"But you do very well for yourself in Bolivia," said Alderete.

"I'm not complaining. I work very hard."

"And what do you do, if I may ask?"

"I'm a promoter. You know that very well. Didn't my girl Lucy explain that to you?"

Alderete's smile vanished.

"Which Lucy is this?" asked Gulietta.

"I don't remember," said Alderete.

"Lucy, the girl from Concepción. The blonde who braided her hair to appear more like a schoolgirl. A lot of people look for images of youth in their erotic fantasies."

"I've heard about that," said Gulietta.

Fire seemed to be coming from Alderete's eyes. But he was no dragon out of Celtic or Anglo-Saxon lore; he was more like a figure on one of those ancient Peruvian gourds, possessing a strange and perverse sensuality.

"My God!" said Doña Clara. "Are there really men like that?"

"Doña Clarita, you have no idea how far men can go with these fantasies. If I only told you—"

"Better you not say anything," interrupted Alderete. "We're in the presence of a young woman who isn't even nineteen years old."

"Don't worry about me," said Gulietta.

"In Buenos Aires, people think differently. Here we don't accept that kind of talk," said Alderete.

"Sex is a fashionable subject in high society," responded Anita.

"In the Tabarís," said Alderete. "Not here."

"Don't get worked up, Don Alde, you might get sick," said Anita.

"Speaking of the Tabarís, the Marquis and his good-for-nothing pals invited me to play a round of poker after dinner."

"You're going to play with those people who don't like you?" asked Anita.

"They like me . . . they'd like to see me screwed," answered Alderete.

"Please," said Doña Clara. "No swearing."

"I want that pimp Tréllez to play. I suspect a little plot. But I'll skin them alive, just as I once did to that clown Ruiz."

"Don't talk about people that way," said Gulietta.

"Ruiz is and always will be a bum."

They savored the dessert, a chocolate mousse with flourishes of whipped cream, the chef's special recipe. Despite the altitude, Alderete was still able to exercise his imagination. "That Durbin guy is there. He's a fourth-class Irishman. He works for the railway and he's traveling with the hag he has for a wife."

"Where is she?" asked Doña Clara.

"In their cabin. She never goes out; she spends all her time reading the Bible."

"And that Russian, Petko. Isn't he the banker for the Jews in La Paz?" asked Anita.

"A fine group," commented Gulietta. "They're all fond of you."

Alderete nodded. "When you climb to the top like me, it's not surprising that a lot of people get envious."

"They're good people. You'll see—after the first drink you'll be friends," said Anita.

"The wine has whetted my appetite. I'll eat them alive."

They had coffee and an after-dinner drink. Anita thanked them and headed for the Marquis's table.

"That old madam isn't good company for you, darling," said Alderete.

Gulietta gulped several times. Her eyes were burning and her neck was starting to hurt. "She's very well-mannered. I don't see anything bad in her."

"When I say she's bad company, it's because I know her. And I don't like you disagreeing with me. It's becoming an obsession of yours."

"We're just having a conversation," said Doña Clara.

Alderete began listening to the endless chatter coming from the table of his soon-to-be opponents.

Anita had found a space to sit at the adjacent table with the Franciscan and the woman with the dog.

"That priest reminds me of an agitator I met in Catavi," said Alderete.

"I'm really tired," said Gulietta. "If you find me asleep, please don't wake me up."

"What?"

"The altitude. We're approaching 16,000 feet."

"I know."

Gulietta and her mother exchanged conspiratorial glances.

"I feel dizzy," said Gulietta.

"Let's go to bed," said Doña Clara. Her expression was similar to that of a Versailles aristocrat on her way to the guillotine.

"I'm going to fetch the whiskey and my cards." He escorted them to Doña Clara's cabin. Gulietta went inside with her mother.

"I thought you were going to sleep," said Alderete.

"It's early."

"Didn't you say you were tired?"

"Please stop watching over me as if you're my stepfather."

Alderete found the whiskey but not the cards. He was certain that he had brought them; he never went anywhere without his cards. They were his good luck charm. He turned the cabin upside down searching for them, but not a trace.

That Solares idiot didn't put them in my suitcase, he thought. *I'll just have to play with Ruiz's cards. If he marked them, it'll be easy to tell.*

Ricardo was lying in wait at his table. He planned to see Gulietta while Alderete was playing cards. No woman had ever turned him on like this before. He couldn't think about anything but her; it was impossible to get her out of his mind. He couldn't stop imagining her fondling him.

Ricardo approached Father Moreno, who was now talking with Carla Marlene. Underneath the table, the contortionist was tickling one of his calves. As the train neared the border, the union leader seemed to be losing his fear of being recognized and his movements became looser and more playful.

"I want to ask you another favor," said Ricardo.

"Let me guess."

"What time are you thinking of going to bed?"

"When the card game is over."

"Sure?"

"Would you doubt the word of a poor follower of Saint Francis, Carla Marlene?" asked Moreno, looking at her.

The contortionist held out her hand to Ricardo.

"This young man caught us," said Moreno.

"Oh really?"

"He saw everything."

Carla Marlene let out a mischievous laugh. "Everything?"

"Well," said Ricardo, "I saw some and imagined the rest."

"We're a couple," explained Carla Marlene.

Father Moreno nodded, without too much fervor.

"We're getting married in Chile," she said.

"You're lucky," said Ricardo.

Carla Marlene suddenly stiffened. "I'm afraid of the dark. There's nobody out there. If we get stopped, no one will help us."

"So, can I count on you, Father?" Ricardo said, ignoring her.

Then, with a look of phony naïvete, Carla Marlene asked Ricardo whom he planned to take to the cabin.

"I guess I don't have a choice," Moreno said.

Ricardo left the dining car as Alderete was making his way in with a bottle of whiskey under his arm. Alderete tried to challenge him with a stare; Ricardo passed so close that he could smell the accountant's cheap cologne, but he simply ignored the man and headed to his own cabin. Alderete watched Ricardo's steps like a hunter; upon seeing him enter his cabin, Alderete continued straight ahead to the poker players' table.

Moments later, Ricardo emerged from his cabin and knocked on the Alderetes' door. He waited for a moment and then continued over to Doña Clara's.

"Hi," he greeted Gulietta. "Aren't you going to watch the card game?"

"I'll wait for you," she said in a hushed voice.

"Who is it?" asked Doña Clara.

"Ricardo; he's come to say goodbye."

Gulietta kissed him cautiously. "I'll see you in a bit."

"Good night, Doña Clara," said Ricardo.

Back in the corridor, the steward was sipping maté tea from a gourd, Argentine-style. Ricardo removed a fifty-peso bill from his wallet and placed it in the upper pocket of the steward's jacket.

"What's this for?"

"You'll let me know when her husband comes back."

"That's very risky, young man. Don't get yourself into trouble. He's a brute. He might kill you."

"It's worth it," said Ricardo.

"To be frank with you, I won't have time." He tried to return the money, but Ricardo stopped him.

"It doesn't matter. If you can, great . . . if not . . ."

Ricardo didn't have to wait long. No sooner had he entered the cabin than Gulietta arrived and flipped on the small light above the sink. A tenuous glow illuminated the contours of the room. They could barely see each other, and this enhanced the ambience of tense sexual excitement. Ricardo removed her sweater and placed it on the upper bunk. He went about unbuttoning her blouse with the stealth of a safe-cracker.

"Can you take off my pants?" he asked.

"Is that what I'm supposed to do?"

"French women do it. I've seen it before in movies."

Gulietta obeyed. The only sound was that of the wind striking the window with unusual force.

She was still wearing panties and a bra. Her body exuded a fresh, pungent scent. Gulietta nimbly climbed the ladder and Ricardo followed, trembling. He stared at her pinkish-white bottom in the dim light as she ascended, the sight of which rendered him incapable of breathing calmly.

"It feels wonderful to be up so high. It makes this very special," said Gulietta.

They covered themselves with the gray blanket provided by the railway. Their lips touched, cautiously at first and then excitedly. She emitted faltering moans and he started to pant like a bicycle racer. He took one of her hands and showed her the way. It was the first time she had caressed the embodiment of a man's energy and desire. She understood that he was offering her the symbol of his virility, the very part which used to inspire laughter and dirty talk at bedtime with her classmates at boarding school in Buenos Aires. Curled up against him, her naked body looked completely vulnerable.

"I'm more nervous than I was this afternoon."

"Don't worry about the priest. He's watching the poker game and your husband is up against a pack of revenge-thirsty dogs."

Alderete trusted his lucky stars. He knew the coalition of rancorous men before him was eager to rip him off mercilessly. Even so, he wasn't afraid; he was difficult to take down in poker.

"Good evening," he said as he approached.

"Don Nazario," replied Ruiz with a hint of sarcasm, "are you itching for a fight?"

"Where should I sit?"

"In back, Don Nazario," said Ruiz in an angelic voice.

Alderete set the bottle of whiskey on top of the table. "We'll start with this one, and then you guys can order a second. If we make it to a third, we'll split the cost."

Petko looked perturbed as he made room for Nazario to squeeze by. The Marquis, Durbin, and Tréllez were seated at the other side of the table, and Petko and Ruiz were in front. The table was made of imported wood and its smooth top shone.

"The cards?"

"You do not trust," said Petko as Alderete examined the deck with great care.

"I know who I'm playing with," responded Alderete.

"Maybe *we* should be the ones saying that," said Durbin.

"It looks like these haven't been marked," said Alderete. "How's everything at the Jewish bank?"

"I am not banker," answered Petko.

"Actually, I've always wondered what you do for a living," said Alderete.

"It does not matter," said Petko. "We came to play cards."

Tréllez served the whiskey.

"It's not just any drink," said Alderete. "Top-shelf Scotch."

"Top or not top, whiskey is whiskey," said Petko.

The person with the highest card would go first. Durbin drew an ace.

Anita settled in at the table in back, escorted by the Franciscan and Carla Marlene. Alderete noticed Father Moreno.

"Isn't your twin brother a union leader?"

Father Moreno turned pale; Carla Marlene pinched his backside.

"You're obsessed," said the priest.

"I'm good with faces," said Alderete.

Durbin dealt the cards with flair. His green eyes avoided looking at Alderete's face; it would unleash his memory and this wasn't a good moment to hash over the past.

From her vantage point, Anita had a full view of Alderete's hand. A rectangular mirror also reflected the hands of Ruiz and Petko. Anita had been instructed to memorize Alderete's cards and, through the use of sign language, send messages to the rest of the players, except for Petko, who wasn't participating in the plot to take down Alderete.

The poker theatrics kicked off with a toast, which was followed by the first squabbling. Durbin raised his glass and proposed a drink to the Republic of Ireland.

Everyone agreed except for Alderete. "The Irish are the ones who always take a beating from the English, right?"

"There's a kind of civil war between the Catholics and the Protestants in Northern Ireland," Durbin clarified.

"I can never tell the difference between the ones from the north and your kind."

"It's because you're ignorant and you don't know the history."

"Don't insult me, goddamnit!" snapped Alderete.

"If you want, we can fix this some other way," suggested Durbin.

"Señores, please. We just started the game, and here we are, about to come to blows. Let's play like civilized people," Ruiz interjected.

"A toast to my wife, who will make me happy for the rest of my days," said Alderete as he sipped on his drink.

The Marquis laughed and Durbin pretended to have a coughing fit.

"What are you laughing about?" demanded Alderete.

"These guys laugh everything, *khuya*," said Petko.

The first few hands favored Alderete: simple three-of-a-kinds and two pairs. His expression resembled a smile, but also conveyed a coldness reminiscent of a rabid mastiff. A second round of drinks was served. Petko was working on a straight; lady luck shined on him and he drew just the card he needed.

Alderete had three aces. Petko balked at Alderete's thousand-peso wager. Anita winked at him, but Petko was playing by the books.

"*Khuya*, I not want these things," he said.

"What things?" asked Alderete.

"Petko's talking to himself," said Tréllez.

"Because nobody's listening, just like when you talk in Congress."

"At least I speak proper Spanish," said Tréllez, "and not some nouveau riche slang."

Petko upped the bet five hundred pesos. Alderete hesitated and scrutinized Petko's face in the hope of finding some trace of a bluff. Petko was staring at his cards without raising his gaze. Alderete matched his bet.

Petko held out his straight. "Go ahead and top that."

Alderete examined the cards one by one. He threw his three aces on the table, served himself another whiskey, called the waiter over, and asked for ice. The waiter headed to the kitchen and they could hear him chopping up ice in a bucket.

"Deal," said Durbin. "When this guy doesn't want to listen, he won't even hear his own conscience."

"I'll do it," said Alderete, ignoring Durbin.

They handed him the cards. Alderete shuffled them several times.

"Not go overboard," advised Petko. "We not cheaters."

"I know what I'm doing. Cut," said Alderete.

The Marquis performed two cuts and handed the cards back to Alderete, who had started whistling a popular tune.

"I like it when you're happy, Nazario," said Ruiz.

"That's Don Nazario to you," said Alderete. "When did I give you permission to call me *tú*?"

Ruiz bit his tongue. Alderete dealt the cards with an exasperating slowness.

"How is it that you all ended up on the same train?" Alderete asked.

"It's vacation season," said the Marquis.

"Don't make me laugh, *you* on vacation?"

"You were on vacation once in Valparaíso," said the Marquis. "You stayed at my house almost a whole month. Don't you remember?"

Alderete ignored him and scrutinized his hand. He had pairs of tens and eights. The Marquis also drew pairs, but his were queens and jacks. Petko had five different cards, and Durbin held pairs of kings and aces. Tréllez held a straight and Ruiz, three nines. They all asked for more cards, except Tréllez. Alderete received an eight, the Marquis a card that was of no use. Petko salvaged a pair; Ruiz cursed the card that Alderete had dealt him. Durbin, to his relief, got a magnificent and unexpected king. Alderete removed a handful of bills from his inner coat pocket and counted two thousand pesos. Durbin raised his cards so Anita could see them. With a quick peep, she spotted Alderete's full house, then patted her own back, indicating that Durbin could bet.

Durbin raised the bar to three thousand pesos. Alderete guessed that the Irishman was bluffing. Tréllez folded.

"Five hundred on top of Durbin's three thousand," Alderete wagered after a long pause.

"Let's see 'em," said Durbin.

Alderete swore when Durbin revealed his hand.

The train came to a halt at the Campero station—another abandoned settlement in the middle of the Andean plain. It was drizzling, and aside from the railway building there was no other light in the area. The train woke the dogs, eliciting a chorus of barks; the local railway employee was sporting a rubber poncho and a sombrero. The engineer, Quispe, got out to stretch his legs and inspected the engine with a lantern. Meanwhile, the card game continued amid misunderstandings, arguments, and caustic remarks. The group had finished a bottle of Scotch and everyone was a little tipsy. Alderete won some hands, lost others, and the plot to clear him out had not yet acquired any momentum.

This was because he hadn't yet consumed enough whiskey to lose control of his emotions, at which point he would become dangerous and vulnerable. With the alcohol rising to his head, however, Alderete, the ex-accountant-turned-bourgeois-gentleman-miner, was beginning to uproot hidden feelings from deep inside his tension-ridden soul. He was returning to his humble origins, not with nostalgia or tenderness but with rage. He was becoming sharp-tongued and sarcastic. This is what his tablemates were waiting for, except for Petko, who remained focused on the game and unaware of what was being stirred up around him.

"Why are we stopping?" asked Alderete.

"The engine has to rest," said Ruiz.

"What the hell do you know about engines?" Alderete countered mockingly.

"I travel to Chile and Argentina all the time."

"Just to rip off idiots on the train. People know about you. One of these days the police will catch you."

"I don't do anything illegal," said Ruiz.

The Marquis sent the cards flying gracefully down onto the table. Alderete drew four jacks. Before he could pull them up against his chest, Anita glimpsed his hand—Alderete would bet until the bitter end. Anita Romero had not only worked as a hostess, a whore, and a madam, she was also a bit of a magician. When she saw the Marquis's troubled gaze, she worked out a way to tip him off to Alderete's hand. The Marquis made use of his knee and Durbin took the hint. He in turn passed the warning on to Tréllez, who at that moment was deep in the red. They needed four queens, four kings, or four aces to beat Alderete's four jacks.

Ruiz got the message as well and four majestic queens sprung forth under the table for precisely the person who needed them. Tréllez already had two queens and tacked on two more as a gift. The smoke from Petko's cigar was a formidable curtain that helped shroud hand and eye movements.

In a ploy to confuse the others, Alderete asked for a card and started mixing it with the rest of his hand. He trusted that another player would open the pot; his hope became reality when Petko, who had garnered a three-of-a-kind, opened with a bet of five hundred pesos, setting off the boom of the night—and everyone got into the mix.

"One thousand over his five hundred," said Alderete.

The ex-accountant's enemies sensed that the trap was set and that the fox was about to step on shaky ground. The five of them each tossed another thousand pesos into the pot.

Tréllez studied his cards once again, lining them up in his left hand while, with his right, holding up an extremely long cigarette in a mother-of-pearl holder. He furrowed his brow and smiled like a giddy young boy who had just come across a photo of a naked woman.

Everyone raised the pot an additional three thousand. The Marquis watched the pile of money with a certain eagerness. "Two thousand more on top of the three thousand," he said.

"Too much for me. I am out," announced Petko.

Durbin, Ruiz, and Alderete placed bets.

"Why don't we up it five thousand?" said Alderete.

A circle of onlookers formed around the table.

"Alderete's five thousand and another ten thousand," said Tréllez.

Durbin and Alderete answered the challenge.

"Better yet, twenty thousand," declared Alderete as he laid out the money.

Durbin produced twenty thousand pesos in brand-new bills, a reflection of the inflationary spiral afflicting Bolivia. Tréllez followed suit and added: "Twenty thousand plus thirty more."

Alderete glanced over at Durbin.

"That's it for me," announced the Irishman.

"Frenchie Tréllez's thirty plus twenty more," said Alderete.

"Better a Frenchie than a pillager of mines," answered Tréllez.

"Are you betting or not?"

"Fifty thousand pesos on top of this squirt's twenty," said Tréllez.

"Where did you get the money?"

"What is it to you?"

"I'll match it," said Alderete. "I'd like to see you call me a squirt again later."

Alderete displayed four jacks and Tréllez, with a princelike gesture, revealed four beautiful queens.

Alderete looked like a sand sculpture being slowly washed away by ocean waves. Overcome by a rush of cold sweat and a sudden spell of rage, he began to break down. "That's impossible!"

"What's impossible?"

"I thought I saw another queen somewhere else," said Alderete.

"You can see what you want to see," replied Durbin. "Are you calling us cheaters?"

"I want to count the queens," he said, his eyes red with anger. They handed him the cards. He searched for the cursed queens, but found only the four. "I saw one more. I won't be played for a fool."

"It could be altitude," said Petko. "Maybe you see things that do not exist."

"Stay out of this. Damn Russian ex-pat; it's too bad the communists didn't catch you."

"*Khuya*, bastard. I Russian émigré, but honorable; difference is you want be white, but nature cannot make miracles like that."

Alderete went searching again for the card under the table.

"You look ridiculous," said the Marquis.

"Nobody messes with me. It's not about the money. I just won't stand for looking like a fool."

"You are fool even if not lose at cards," said Petko.

Alderete forced the other players to rummage through their pockets, setting off an uproar of laughter. Their trusted ally, Anita, began her retreat. Even though he looked as if he were suffering from a seizure, Alderete happened to notice the mirror at his back. He stood up and went over to the table where Father Moreno and Carla Marlene were still seated.

"A perfect view," he said. "It was a damn conspiracy."

Father Moreno was transformed into a dummy observing the scene with a look of infantile obliviousness.

"Do you know something about this?" asked Alderete.

"About what?" answered Moreno.

"You're no priest. I'm going to have the police get you in Charaña."

"You're always threatening people," said Carla Marlene. "Who do you think you are?"

"Are you talking to me?" asked Alderete.

"What do you think?"

"This won't be the end of it," said Alderete.

"It's over," said Tréllez. "You're a sore loser."

"Loser, my balls. I want my money back," growled Alderete.

They laughed in unison, and Tréllez warned: "Don't forget that I'm a congressman with the PURS. My authority ends only at the border. No more shouting, no more fucking around with me. You should be happy you didn't lose any more money. Durbin wants to beat you to a pulp."

"He's a foreigner," said Alderete. "If he touches me I'll complain to the authorities."

"I'd like to see that," said Durbin. "Once we're in Chilean territory, I'll break your fingers one by one."

Alderete contained his aggression. The had obviously ganged up against him and further prodding could only stir up more trouble. Yet the whiskey, the jousting, and the smirking faces of his rivals only increased the tension. A bout of chills and dizziness came over him. He prepared his retreat, trying to keep from looking like a fool. But the commotion at the table raged on. Although they contradict the commandments of the Holy Catholic Church, acts of vengeance, however small, are nearly always deeply satisfying.

The train was robbing empty space from the Altiplano. The darkness became oppressive. The flats had an otherworldly look to them;

even the toughest shrubs grew with difficulty. Alderete summoned his courage and began walking toward his cabin. The narrow passage between the tables seemed endless. More laughter and jeers erupted from the crew of swindlers.

"We're coming into a station," said Ricardo.

Gulietta couldn't really hear what he was saying. She felt as if Ricardo was strangling her, as if his lips wouldn't let her breathe. They quivered awkwardly at first, then slackened and began mumbling something unintelligible. Ricardo was trying to get into just the right position. After pinning down her arms, he kissed her on the forehead and penetrated with a hard thrust, forcing out a cry that became confused with the engine's heavy breathing.

The engineer could be overheard talking outside. In the corridor, the watchman shouted something that Ricardo thought was a warning. He moved his body haltingly until she allowed herself to lie still and relax, at which point his gyrations acquired a more rhythmic pattern. He looked at Gulietta's face, a mixture of pain and passion. Even though she hadn't said a word, she was writing poetry with her eyes. She began scratching Ricardo's back delicately, while her legs propped him up and pulled him deeper inside.

The wild barking of stray dogs sounded in the night. Cold breezes entered through cracks in the window and under the door.

"Why are you stopping?" asked Gulietta.

"That engineer is making me nervous."

"Keep going. Why do you care?"

Gulietta clung to him as if she were some sort of space monster that lived off the blood of humans. She initiated a dance without pauses and he gracelessly tried to follow her lead. Gulietta felt an almost unbearable pain, as if a burning hot knife were stabbing into her vagina. She still wasn't sure whether or not she had lost her virginity, but she sensed that Ricardo was afraid of something.

"Don't worry about what's going on outside."

A series of spasms ran up and down her spine; she was very wet and wanted to keep going for a long time.

Ricardo stared at her lovingly, but all she wanted was to feel him deep inside, invading her completely. Love didn't matter to her in that moment, just the suffering that was ripping through her.

Footsteps reverberated in the hallway and Ricardo got ahold of himself. "The watchman's going away."

They switched positions. Gulietta got on top and started to gallop forcefully. She touched herself and moaned; the pain was turning her on even more.

Gulietta found that she couldn't stop. She had thrown herself down a slope full of colors, shapes, and sensations. Even though Ricardo had dominated her at first, now he was little more than a marionette. He had no other choice but to leave his penis in the flag position.

She's going to destroy it, she's skinning me alive, he thought. He wanted to ask her to slow down a little, but her utterances seemed to be devouring all time and space.

A whistle from the engine became one with Gulietta's cry, a cry of victory, happiness, and revenge. Ricardo climaxed too, but fearfully, tormented by his partner's momentum. This was just what she wanted: an orgasm that felt like being inside a hurricane, like the pain of giving birth and the anguish of sin. He felt he had been used somehow, but he knew he had agreed to be the guinea pig, and now here he was, covered in Gulietta's tears and his own sweat.

"That was really beautiful," she said.

"Yeah, really beautiful," he replied with little conviction.

"I hope there's blood," she said.

"What for?"

"What do you mean *what for?* If there's no blood, then it wasn't consummated."

"Where'd you hear that?"

"My mother told me there's supposed to be blood the first time."

Ricardo felt cold and started to tremble. She wasn't getting up. She was still sitting on top of him, striking a dominant, contented pose.

"If he finds out, I think he's going to kill me," she said.

"Keep him guessing."

"It wasn't as good as you'd hoped?"

"It was much better," he said.

"You're not lying?"

"Do I look like a liar?"

"You look like a crybaby," she said. "I think you're scared."

"Scared?"

"That Nazario will show up."

Gulietta's satisfaction was complete once she verified that a long, bright-red bloodstain adorned the bedsheet.

"*Here it is, the proof of the crime,*" she said in English.

"The only thing missing is the angry victim, his suffering, his outrage. He deserves it," said Ricardo.

Gulietta threw off the bedsheet and flaunted her stunning figure, which, until just an hour before, had been shrouded in an aura of innocence. The sweat drenching her body conferred upon her an extraordinary sensuality.

"Now you're a real woman."

"Enough with the cheesy clichés. I wish we could do it again," she said.

"Give me some room to breathe. Besides, we don't have much time."

"Because of the priest?"

"He's not a problem anymore."

"Is he very liberal?"

"He's not a priest."

"Then why does he wear robes?"

"He's running from the law. He's a labor union leader. Some of those guys are behind bars, you know."

"He's really something."

"Keep it to yourself. I gave him my word that I wouldn't open my mouth. I saw that contortionist go under his robes once: You can imagine what for."

"Oh really? Which one is the contortionist?"

"She's the one with the dog, the one with the beautiful knockers."

Gulietta cupped one of her breasts with her hand.

"What about mine?"

"They're perfect."

"Can't you do it again right now?"

"I have to . . . warm up again; let's say fifteen minutes."

"It takes you that long?"

"Sometimes less, sometimes more, it depends on the girl."

"I hope you set a new record with me."

"So . . . this isn't one of your dangerous days?"

"I don't know."

"What?"

"What does it matter? I'd like to have your baby." She started fondling him, verifying that his equipment was at rest after a long battle.

Suddenly, footsteps sounded in the adjacent cabin.

"He's back," whispered Gulietta. "Sooner than I expected. Maybe he's looking for something and he'll turn around and leave."

"I can't sleep in sheets like this," said Ricardo, abruptly but quietly changing the subject. "I'll give the steward a good tip so he can bring me new ones."

"I'll hold onto it," said Gulietta.

Ricardo let out a chuckle of surprise.

"I'll cut out the part with the blood on it. You can just buy the sheet from him."

"Possibly."

"Do it. That way I can have something to remember you by forever. I want to remember you just as you are at this moment."

"You're being too melodramatic."

There were several knocks on the door. The two of them shuddered. Ricardo got down from his bunk and opened the door cautiously.

"Alderete is looking for his wife. He went into Doña Clara's cabin," whispered the steward.

"What!" Gulietta exclaimed.

"He's looking for you," said Ricardo.

"I'll get dressed."

Alderete exited Doña Clara's cabin, beside himself. He may have had a poor imagination, but his gut almost never failed him. His instinct told him that his wife was visiting cabin number six, the one with the rich brat.

"Is she in there?" he asked the steward.

The steward could do little but nod his head; fear sometimes trumps our best intentions. Alderete threw himself against the cabin door.

He was clearly unprepared for the scene that unraveled before him. A more sophisticated spirit might have discerned its unique iconographical appeal, but Alderete was a simple man.

"Son of a bitch!"

He stood silently in the middle of the room, while Ricardo seized the moment to yank on his trousers and Gulietta her panties, which hung suggestively from a clothes hook next to the bunk. Alderete clutched his neck with both hands; he was short of breath.

In the dim light of the cabin, it was impossible to distinguish exactly what was going on with Alderete, but the man was having problems. He turned around and staggered into the corridor. The steward saw this and locked himself up inside his booth. The cold was intense, and the train's swaying made it hard for Alderete to get his balance. He entered his own cabin, unbuttoned his shirt, and undid his tie. He looked for his flask of water on top of the washbowl and took one long swig, then another. He lay down on the mattress and tried to ring the bell to call the steward, but he didn't have the energy. His eyesight clouded up and a sharp, searing pain crossed his forehead. He was unable to shout. He opened his mouth, but no sound came out. He took a deep breath and tried to calm down. His heart wouldn't listen; it continued racing. It was a good thing somebody showed up at his side. Alderete didn't recognize who it was; he could only make out that it was a man.

"I don't have much time," said the figure as he sat down on the bed.

"Are you the steward?"

"No."

"Who are you?"

"Your half-brother, Rocha, the cripple, the one you left without half a leg."

"Rocha? What are you doing on this train?"

"I'm your traveling companion. Death sent me as a messenger."

"What do you want?"

"Guess."

"Call for help; I feel sick. I'll give you money."

Rocha smiled and flaunted his naked stub. Then Alderete noticed that Rocha had become motionless. He was contemplating something else in a distant world.

"What are you going to do?"

With a catlike swipe, Rocha covered Alderete's nose and mouth with a rag. He raised his head and started to count. Alderete flailed at Rocha's body with both arms, but it was no use. He didn't even have time to say the Lord's Prayer before he stopped breathing.

To be thorough, Rocha kept his hand over Nazario's face a few minutes more, completely asphyxiating him. *This chump might be faking it*, he thought.

But Alderete wasn't faking anything. He was as dead as a fish in an icebox. Rocha stood up and opened the door with extreme caution. Fortunately, the corridor was now empty. He steadied himself on his crutches and returned to his cabin, then uncapped the *pisco* and downed what was left in a single gulp.

"Well," he said out loud, "I didn't do so badly. The bastard's in hell, where he always belonged."

Rocha broke out in a strange step that could have passed for a primitive African dance. He struck at the floor with his crutches à la Long John Silver, his favorite fictional character.

Rocha was gleeful; for the first time in his life, he had seen something through to a happy ending. It had all gone exactly according to plan. Nobody had seen him enter or leave the cabin. Poor Nazario had died from some sort of attack—a heart attack at that altitude was always possible. Especially for someone with high blood pressure.

They finished getting dressed in silence. Gulietta thought about how her mother would react. Alderete would probably ask for a divorce, or, at the very least, he would cancel the trip and separate from her, rendering null and void the transfer documents for the house in Obrajes, the lots in Miraflores, and the warehouse on Yungas Street. The same went for Doña Clara's pension and the other terms of the marriage arrangement. She had ruined everything in less than three days; her mother would never forgive her.

"What will you do?" asked Ricardo.

"I'll see my mother and then I'll face him."

"He looked sick," said Ricardo. "It seemed like he was about to have a heart attack; otherwise I'm sure he would have hit me. I was afraid he'd come back with a gun. He still might. Have you seen a weapon anywhere?"

"No. He would have come back by now. It's been more than five minutes. I think he's waiting in the cabin for me to give him some kind of explanation, but what can I say, he caught us in bed . . ."

"You could say nothing happened."

"Don't be naïve. We were both naked. What would I tell him? That we were having a competition to see who can get dressed faster?"

"That steward is an idiot."

"You're acting like a baby, Ricardo. What's done is done and we have to face the consequences. Nothing will happen to you. Are you afraid?"

Ricardo felt like his balls were stuck in his throat.

"No, not afraid . . ." he stammered.

"Then so what? I'm my own person. And the sheet, you can keep it," said Gulietta as she got ready to leave.

"Sheet? What sheet?"

Gulietta ignored his question and walked out.

Doña Clara was reading a book by her favorite author, Vicky Baum, when her daughter entered her cabin.

"He caught us," Gulietta said.

"Doing what?"

"You know . . ."

"I don't know anything."

"I warned you that he wouldn't be my first."

"In bed?"

"Yes."

"Goodness, and what did he say?"

"He froze, then he grabbed his throat and took off. He looked like he was in a state of shock."

"I can imagine. And now . . . ?"

"I'm sorry, Mamá. I couldn't . . . I just couldn't . . ." Gulietta started crying inconsolably.

Doña Clara stood up and hugged her. "Well, it had to happen someday. It's too bad it was so fast. There wasn't even time to fix the papers."

"If he wants a divorce, he'll have to give me something," said Gulietta.

"Adultery is a strike against you. *In the act*. He caught you in the act. There would have to be witnesses for our side."

"There's Ricardo."

"Ricardo was in on it."

"The steward? We could probably buy him off."

"So could Alderete. He has more money."

Doña Clara slipped a shawl over her shoulders, closed her book, and took Gulietta by the hand. "Let's go see him. And Ricardo?"

"I don't know. He was getting dressed."

The corridor was empty and the wind was howling. The light rain had ceased, but its passing made the air feel even colder. Doña Clara pushed open the door to Alderete's cabin, which was dark inside. She turned on the ceiling light and discovered Nazario lying flat on his back on the bed, his eyes wide open. She hurried up to him and touched his face with the palm of her hand.

"He's lukewarm . . . Nazario?"

No answer.

"Are you okay?" asked Doña Clara.

"Mamá! Take his pulse!"

Doña Clara unbuttoned his shirt, lifted his undershirt, and pressed her ear against his chest. Not even Alderete's soul could be heard.

"Call Tréllez," Doña Clara said.

"Is he dead?"

"I don't know."

"My God!"

The dining car was officially closed, but Gulietta could see Tréllez at the table living it up with the others. Everyone was sitting there, including the Franciscan and Carla Marlene. One of the waiters let Gulietta pass when he noticed how distressed she was.

"Gulietta," said Tréllez, "you look like you've seen a ghost."

"It's my husband. I think he's had a heart attack."

Tréllez was drunk and struggled to stand up. "Excuse me, Gulietta, but we were celebrating."

Upon seeing how upset Gulietta was, Anita woke Moreno, who had dozed off. The two of them, along with Carla Marlene and Tréllez, followed Gulietta to the cabin.

"Lose at cards mess up his head," said Petko. "Fake attack to get attention. That jerk is just fine."

The Marquis looked like a figure out of the Fallas Festival in Spain. The whiskey had caused his enormous nose to turn red. "What could be wrong with the guy?"

"He just wants people to feel sorry for him," said Ruiz.

Moments later, however, Tréllez confirmed that Alderete had passed on to a better life. While he had never liked the man, the PURS congressman got choked up. "Give him the blessing," he told the priest.

Father Moreno smiled beatifically.

"Don Tréllez is a congressman with the ruling party," Carla Marlene explained.

The Franciscan descended from heaven to earth. They were still an hour or two away from the border; if Tréllez realized that Moreno was an activist, he could have him put behind bars in Charaña. He had no choice but to go look for his worn Bible. He returned a few minutes later accompanied by Ricardo, who was pale as a fallen leaf.

"What happened?" Ricardo asked Gulietta.

"He died."

"From the shock?"

"What shock?" asked Tréllez.

Ricardo went mute like a defendant hearing his death sentence.

"Alderete was very upset about losing the game," said Doña Clara.

"We'd better tell the truth . . . He found me and Ricardo in the cabin."

"I see." Tréllez shut Alderete's eyelids. "Father?"

"Let us pray," said Father Moreno. "Bildad's First Speech, in the book of Job: *For we are but of yesterday, and know nothing, because our days upon earth are a shadow . . .* And from Proverbs: *It is better to dwell in the wilderness than with a contentious and angry wife.*"

Carla Marlene kicked him in the ankle.

"Let us say the Lord's Prayer," sputtered Father Moreno.

Everyone gathered together and recited the prayer, following along with affected unction. Father Moreno appeared a bit shaken.

For his part, Ricardo went from surprise to despair; he was absolutely certain that the sight of his and Gulietta's transgression had caused Nazario's fatal attack. Though Ricardo clearly had no fondness for him—he had slept with Alderete's brand-new wife while he was playing cards, after all—his antipathy hadn't reached such a level that he wished him dead.

Watching her husband grow stiff, Gulietta was seized by a flood of emotions. In all sincerity, she believed he didn't deserve this, that the punishment was excessive. Yet after a few minutes had passed, she calmed down and concluded it was the best thing that could have happened. Death had visited the accountant at just the right moment. The night had looked very bleak, with Alderete so worked up over his wife's rejection in addition to his loss and humiliation at the card table.

Doña Clara, being a practical woman, joined Alderete's hands over his chest and, together with Anita, went about fixing him up in the appropriate manner. They combed his hair and arranged his head on the pillow. Alderete now appeared to be sleeping. His facial features seemed to relax, giving off a peaceful aura which clearly moved the other passengers—something he had never been able to do while alive.

The Marquis entered the room. His expression was devoid of emotion. He gazed at Nazario, verified that he was truly dead, then turned toward Doña Clara. "If the Chileans see he's dead, they'll send him back. It's one thing for a live person to pass, but a corpse is something else entirely."

"Please don't talk like that," said Doña Clara.

"Well . . . that's the way it is. You two would have to spend the night in Charaña and then return to La Paz."

"What a pain!" said Gulietta.

"And now what do we do?" asked Doña Clara.

"The best thing would be to . . ." The Marquis closed the door and invited Father Moreno and Carla Marlene to listen to him closely. "You mustn't tell anyone about what happened. The Chilean border guards would hold us up all night. You know how they are; just like the Prussians. You can't reason with them. Better if this goes unnoticed."

"How?" asked Father Moreno.

The Marquis approached Doña Clara, who had started cleaning Nazario's face with a cream. "The best thing would be for him to sleep in peace," he said.

"Then we won't spend the night here with him?" asked Doña Clara.

"That depends on you. My advice would be to let him sleep like an angel, and tomorrow morning, once we're in Chile, you sound the alarm. Gulietta can get out of bed and mourn like Mary Magdalene."

"I won't sleep here," insisted Gulietta.

"Poor girl," said the Marquis. "Just married and with a dead man already on her back."

Doña Clara asked Father Moreno and Carla Marlene to leave the cabin. "Don't ever mention what happened," she said.

"Don't worry," replied Father Moreno. "We'll be as silent as a tomb."

"Marquis, what will become of Nazario's fortune?" asked Doña Clara.

"According to the law, Gulietta is the legitimate heir."

"Doesn't he have children?"

"He had lovers, half-breed girls, and he's probably fathered a kid or two, but I doubt he acknowledged any of them. The money of her husband, may he rest in peace, belongs to Gulietta. There's nothing more to say."

"Do you think God did this?"

"He must have had a hand in it."

"Will we have to undress him?" asked Doña Clara.

"Of course; if you can't handle it, I'll take care of it myself," said Anita.

"No . . . no, I'll help you."

"Here's the plan," said the Marquis. "The man undresses, gets in bed, and goes to sleep. Tomorrow at around 8, Gulietta will enter the cabin without being seen, and then she'll call the steward. Immediately, at the next station, we'll let the authorities know that Alderete is no longer with us: a heart attack due to his high blood pressure, which was severely aggravated by the altitude."

"Do you think we'll be able to bury him in Arica?" asked Doña Clara.

"In general the Chileans are incorruptible, but there are always those who are capable of turning over the El Morro fortress* to Peru for fifty pounds sterling."

"I'm not going back to La Paz," said Gulietta.

"You'll do what I say."

"Mamá, I'll be a laughingstock!"

"So what? Everybody dies someday."

**A tall, steep hill which, during the War of the Pacific, served as the last bulwark for Peruvian troops who garrisoned the city of Arica against the Chilean army. In one of the war's most famous battles, on June 7, 1880, Chilean troops decisively assaulted and captured the fortress.*

"The Americans have an expression, *Life is hard and then you die,*" said the Marquis.

"You can stay in Arica for a few days," said Ricardo.

Gulietta had forgotten about her newfound lover. "You look so pale."

"How do you want me to look? We shocked him to death."

"Nobody could have known that he'd come into the cabin."

"It was always a possibility," said Ricardo. "I feel bad . . ."

The Marquis took him by the arm. "Ricardo, my friend, you had nothing to do with it. He died all by himself."

"Everybody dies by himself, but we gave him a good shove."

"Shut up, please," said Gulietta.

"Ricardo, you still haven't explained to me what you were doing with my daughter in your cabin."

"I can't believe it. This could be a Billy Wilder comedy," said Ricardo.

"You didn't answer my question," Doña Clara pressed.

Ricardo sat down at Alderete's feet and couldn't contain his laughter.

"It's nerves," said Gulietta.

Ricardo laughed and laughed. He finally calmed down and pinched his cheek. "I'm not dreaming," he said.

There was a knock at the door right then. It was Durbin.

"Come in," said Doña Clara.

Petko, Ruiz, and Lourdes followed Durbin inside. The three men were obviously drunk, while Lourdes possessed the impassivity of an actress in a Greek tragedy.

"Our condolences, Doña Clara," Durbin said, then hugged Gulietta. "I can imagine your pain."

"It all happened so fast," the young girl responded.

"They can't blame us," said Durbin. "He lost fair and square."

"That's not what killed him," said Ricardo.

"Please," said Gulietta. "Don't throw wood on the fire."

Durbin contemplated the dead man indifferently. "All that money. He won't even be able to take his wallet with him."

"Doña Clarita, maybe you can return the land he stole from me," said Ruiz.

"Señor Ruiz, it's only been a few minutes since he left us and you're asking me for your land. Don't you think it's a little premature?"

"Let's not worry about the small things," said Lourdes. "Let's concentrate on his soul."

The Marquis, who seemed to be the unofficial master of ceremonies, spoke in a loud and authoritative tone: "Let's allow Doña Clara, Lourdes, and Anita to undress him and put him in bed. The man needs his sleep."

Petko appeared perplexed and asked what was going on. The Marquis quietly explained the plan.

"It seems like a smart decision," said Tréllez. "Once we're in Arica, maybe Doña Clara can convince the authorities to bury him there. I think we all agree that Alderete should continue the trip tonight. I'll tell the steward the truth, I think we can trust him. He collects the documents and hands them to the Chilean authorities. The Chilean police will come to verify the identity of each passenger. Since Alderete will be asleep, they probably won't bother him. If they do come, Gulietta has to be in the cabin for as long as the operation lasts. Chilean police are respectful."

"The immigration agents in our country generally just take the documents and let the passengers sleep," said the Marquis.

Tréllez called the steward. Leaving his congressional eloquence behind, and in simple terms, he explained to the man what had happened.

"It's dangerous," the steward said. "If he's dead, we can't bring him back to life."

"Anything's possible," countered Tréllez. "Trust me, you have absolutely no responsibility. If you don't know anything, they can't blame you for anything. It's simple."

"I could lose my job," said the steward.

"But I never spoke to you," said Tréllez.

"Really?"

"Listen to me. Go on back to your booth and we'll have an emissary deliver an envelope to you. If what's inside makes you happy, let me know, otherwise it would mean putting this train journey at risk. Police shenanigans can take forever. Besides, I'm an honorable congressman for the PURS and I'll give you my card. If you need anything, you can look for me in Congress."

"I'll be waiting," the steward said.

Tréllez's collection reached the sum of five thousand pesos, a small fortune if you took into account the steward's salary. Ruiz delivered the money to him in a sealed white envelope.

"As far as I'm concerned, Alderete shouldn't be disturbed due to his precarious health," the steward declared after counting the money.

"Say no more . . ."

Lourdes, Anita, and Doña Clara dressed Nazario in his brand-new, bright silk pajamas.

"What were you planning to wear tonight, baby dolls?" Ricardo asked Gulietta.

"Don't be morbid."

They settled him on his side, with his face tilted toward the headboard, then everyone left to go rest. Doña Clara and Gulietta stayed in

Alderete's cabin to check his briefcase, wallet, checkbook . . . in sum, the complete belongings of Don Nazario, who was now being robbed. Of course, Doña Clara and Gulietta added a certain touch and elegance to the operation, but that didn't make the looting any less determined. Besides, Gulietta was the widow and had every right.

"Can I sleep with you, Mamá?" asked Gulietta.

"Of course, darling. I'll watch over your dreams, just like when you were little."

Ricardo strolled slowly around the patch of land where the train had stopped, confused by the string of events that had gotten him into this fix. It was the first time he had ever seen a dead person with whom he had spoken only an hour before. Though impetuous, Ricardo was also a delicate and sensitive young man. Alderete's fatal attack had affected him, and he felt a disturbing tingling sensation deep inside his heart. If the act of love with Gulietta had detonated Alderete's cardiac collapse, Ricardo may not have wielded the dagger, but he had been a participant. Who could assure him that, subconsciously, an intention to cause harm hadn't been there, just waiting to rear its head? Was he in love with Gulietta? These questions churned in his mind as he paced back and forth over that frozen piece of earth. Was it simply lust that had driven him or did he want to go farther with this girl who was married to a man she hated not only as a person but for having been the indirect cause of her own father's death? Nobody would be watching over *his* dreams that night; his nightmares would only be diluted by his insomnia.

Father Moreno, who was ready to change his outfit once they crossed the border, rejected Carla Marlene's proposal to spend the night with him and keep him company during such a special moment. "We're already in Charaña," he said.

The cold was causing the wood-paneled passenger cars to creak. A pair of stray dogs stared at the second-class windows, hoping that some-one would toss them a morsel of bread. Ricardo was surprised to see a gang of boys, who looked about ten or twelve years old, playing soccer at that late hour—the clock would soon strike midnight. The Bolivian border post was illuminated by a dim lightbulb.

The Bolivian policemen, wrapped in enormous ponchos, waited for the railway inspector, who was busy collecting the documents of the second-class passengers.

In the sleeping car, the steward discovered Rocha completely drunk, which surprised him since the man had told him just that morning that he was ill. "I think booze is the best thing for lowering this damn fever," Rocha said upon handing him his passport. He gave him a fifty-peso tip and asked for a jug of water for his hangover.

Father Moreno was still wearing his robes, but behind his smile was the knowledge that he was only two hundred yards away from escaping the Bolivian police, who seemed focused above all on emptying the overnight bags stored under the seats of the second-class passengers.

The inspector ordered one of the cargo cars to be opened, and they found the little dog curled up between some bags. Carla Marlene gave him a piece of bread and a small cup of water.

"He'll hold up," said Father Moreno. "The cold doesn't seem to be getting to him."

"Saint Francis is watching over him," said Carla Marlene.

The inspector's eyes were fixed on Carla Marlene's behind. He closed the gate and, as Father Moreno walked away, whispered into her ear, "If you like, I can get the dog out of here and put him in my cabin."

"How kind of you," said Carla Marlene.

"You can *both* spend the night in my cabin," the man added.

During her circus travels, Carla Marlene had received dozens of similar propositions, but she considered herself an artist and not a cheap whore. "You're very forward," she responded. "Don't forget that there's a priest in our midst."

"And what does that have to do with it?"

"I could tell your bosses about your suggestion."

"Señor Durbin is my boss."

"The Irishman?"

"Yeah, and I guarantee you he won't give a damn," said the inspector.

Carla Marlene swung her hips around and walked away in a huff.

Ricardo reached the platform of the sleeping car and still couldn't get it off his mind . . .

In a worst-case scenario, Ricardo had made a token contribution toward liberating Nazario from the travails of the here and now to enjoy boundless celestial freedom. It was now Ricardo's time to enjoy earthly privileges and the most spectacular ass he had seen in all his adolescent years. Not even the cold of the high plains had extinguished that hope for him.

The train stayed still for another half hour before it would resume its march toward Chilean territory. Passengers' documents were being verified and the policemen escorted a pair of half-breed women who appeared to be concealing contraband to the customs office.

The two women had worried expressions on the way in but were all smiles on the way out, which, simply put, seemed to indicate that their problems had been solved. It wasn't a bad gig to be a customs agent at that border crossing. See something out of line, and fix it just by turning off the light and lifting two or three *pollera* skirts into the air.

In the life of a traveler, the impossible is always possible; everything depends on whether you have enough bills on hand or how badly you want to work out your problems.

"All aboard!" the chief inspector finally shouted.

Quispe, who had been warming up his body with a shot of *aguardiente*, headed back to the locomotive. After three long toots, the train was ready to continue its journey across the imaginary line dividing the two countries. It slowly advanced to the site of the relatively modern building used by Chilean customs. The meticulous and authoritarian Chilean national police were stationed a few yards beyond, in a separate single-story structure. Three of them headed over to the second-class cars and started checking the luggage of the intimidated travelers. After more than twenty minutes, they moved on to the sleeping car. They began in cabin number one, which was Rocha's.

"He's a poor invalid," said the steward. "There's no point in bothering him."

Rocha had been sleeping, and he panicked when he saw the Chilean policemen. But he calmed down when he determined that they were merely checking papers.

"What's wrong with you?" asked one of the policemen.

"I have a fever," Rocha said. His stuttering drunkard's voice had caught the cop's attention. "I drank some *pisco* to make myself sweat."

The Chileans went on to inspect the other cabins. They eventually arrived at Alderete's.

"Señor Alderete suffers from high blood pressure, he's not feeling well," the steward said.

"Open up," one of them ordered.

Inside, on the lower bunk, Alderete appeared to be sleeping so deeply that he didn't hear the cop's imperious voice.

The policeman studied his passport; he wanted to be sure that it was the same guy who was resting motionlessly before him.

"Wake him up," demanded the cop.

At that moment, somebody on the top bunk pulled opened the curtain. It was Gulietta, wearing a nightgown.

"Good evening, sergeant," she said.

"Captain," he clarified.

"Captain, my husband has heart trouble. We got him to sleep with a very strong pill. If he wakes up he'll have a hard time falling back asleep."

"I want to see his face," said the captain as he flipped through the passport.

Gulietta descended and, with the voice of a caring wife, whispered into Alderete's ear: "Honey, they just want to see your face."

The captain bent over slightly. Alderete's face looked like that of a hibernating groundhog. Thankfully, the captain did not notice that he wasn't breathing and bid farewell with a tip of his cap.

Gulietta covered her body with a robe and waited for the other Chilean authorities to leave the car. Seconds later, Doña Clara entered.

"Are you in shock?" asked Doña Clara.

"I feel a mixture of things. I'm not happy that he died. Even though I would have preferred a simple divorce, it would've been very hard for me to put up with him. Every time he touched me, my hair felt like it was standing on end and I wanted to throw up. He wasn't an honorable man, but catching me and Ricardo in the middle of . . ."

"Debauchery."

"It's my fault. It was my idea."

"Will Ricardo talk about his feat?" asked Doña Clara.

"I don't think so. He's upset, and besides, he's a gentleman."

"A gentleman who made love to a lady on her honeymoon."

"He's eighteen years old, Mamá."

"Let's just hope he keeps his mouth shut. Can you make sure of that?"

"Of course."

"I'll take care of the arrangements once we arrive in Arica . . . And, well, that's the end of our problem. I think that your father, may he rest in peace, has been avenged. It was Nazario's destiny not to deflower you."

"Sounds like a cheap novel."

The train headed into Chilean territory. It was impossible to distinguish one landscape from the other; it was all part of the same Andean steppe.

When Anita entered the cabin, Gulietta explained, "They didn't even notice. Imagine that, the captain hardly even bent over to see his face."

"We'll stick to the Marquis's plan," said Doña Clara.

"And you, my dear, will you be returning to La Paz?" asked Anita.

"No," said Gulietta."

"What will you do?"

"I don't know."

"The best thing would be for you to take the *Santa Rita* tomorrow night," Doña Clara advised.

"By myself?"

"By yourself. Aunt Ernestina will be waiting for you in New Orleans. I understand it's a very beautiful city. It was part of France for a long time. The people eat well, and there's the French Quarter. You won't be bored."

"I feel a little bad because of Ricardo," said Gulietta.

"He knew that you would have to leave tomorrow."

"You didn't fall in love with him, did you?" asked Anita.

"I like him, but he's my age."

"Think about enjoying yourself," said Doña Clara. "Let's put this whole train episode behind us."

"I'll set the alarm for 8 o'clock and Gulietta will come back into this cabin without being seen," said Anita.

"I'm afraid," murmured Gulietta. "I've always been afraid of dead people."

"It'll just be for a little while," said Doña Clara. "Later we'll all be there with you. We'll get to the coast before too long."

They retreated to the other cabin and undressed. Anita lay down beside Doña Clara, at her feet, and Gulietta climbed into the upper bunk. The latest turmoil had passed and Gulietta was finally calming down. *I'm free, I'm alone, and I'm rich,* she thought. *I liked what I did with Ricardo a lot; they say you never forget the first time. I feel bad about leaving him tomorrow. It's a little humiliating for him, but like my mom says, he knew what he was getting into.*

Gulietta figured that insomnia would overtake her and she wouldn't get any rest; but the swaying of the train made her drowsy, and after a few minutes she fell asleep.

Edmundo Rocha, meanwhile, was wide awake, gazing at the night sky. Seated in front of his cabin window, he held an envelope in his hand. He had already counted the money three times; a splendid foot tap had slipped it to him under the door. He was dazzled by the sky's unusually starry splendor. The effect of the *pisco* had worn off and he was combating the hangover with a large jug of water. Unlike Ricardo and Gulietta, Rocha felt content. What he had done to Alderete, he had been thinking about doing for years. Yet he had been incapable of doing it alone. He remembered with extraordinary clarity the look on his victim's face, a look at once imploring and questioning, for Alderete hadn't had a lot of time for reflection. Rocha smiled. Things had always been difficult for him, and he squandered nearly every opportunity that presented itself. But he had just delivered a masterful performance, efficient and quick, like a leopard chasing down a gazelle. When the train stopped in Charaña, he had gotten under the covers and waited. His heart beat unusually fast when the Chilean cops entered his cabin; he had thought it was the beginning of another tragedy. Later, he overheard the women talking about Alderete's death. They weren't holding a wake for him, he was sure of that. The corridor was now empty and silent. The train forged ahead.

What would happen now? He would find out tomorrow. The deal had been to kill the guy and stay in his oppressive cabin until they got to Chile. He took off his clothes. He stared at his half-leg for a good while, this time feeling relief instead of anger. With the help of a prosthesis, which he would buy in Chile, it would soon be a full leg, albeit not a normal one. At the very least, it would pass unnoticed by most of the people who normally stared at him, whether out of curiosity or compassion. He turned off the light and hid the envelope with the money under his pillow. Rocha wanted to be exceptional in life, but reality wouldn't let him. He was a sad, lonely drunkard, a creature of habit; nothing special. Now he had become a murderer, somebody definitely out of the ordinary. He had a new feeling since killing Nazario, as if he now belonged to a forbidden cult.

The train was still crossing over the top of the world, but would soon descend toward the coast. Seated on a bench in the engine car, Quispe drank a shot of *pisco* and thought to himself that it was going to be another one of those never-ending nights.

By daybreak, the landscape had changed completely; the train was maneuvering between mountains. A pale red was the dominant color. Sand seemed to be caressing the foot of the mountain range. The warm air announced that they were finally leaving the higher elevations. The train was descending along switchbacks.

Doña Clara woke up very early. She got dressed and entered the cabin next to hers. The train's overnight rocking had straightened Alderete, who was now "sleeping" on his back. Doña Clara returned to her cabin and waited. Gulietta was sound asleep. Doña Clara thought that her face looked beautiful, that she resembled her father, Don Rafael Carletti. She wept for a few moments as she remembered her husband, who had left her without making her happy in the last stage of her life, when she needed him the most.

At 8 o'clock she woke Gulietta. Anita was still enjoying the sleep of a madam without regrets.

"Go to your cabin and lie down for a while on the top bunk. A few minutes later come and see me. Anita and I will make sure the other passengers find out about Alderete's death," Doña Clara said.

"It'll be impossible for me to cry," said Gulietta.

"You never faked crying before?"

"Once, in a play at school."

"Well, then do it again. You don't have to drown us in tears. Just don't wear makeup and look like you're suffering."

The Marquis's instructions were followed to the letter. Gulietta showed up before long in her mother's cabin.

"It's your turn," she said.

Anita and Doña Clara went to the Marquis's cabin to rouse him. He took all the time in the world to groom himself.

"Please hurry," said Doña Clara. "We have to dress him and start the wake."

"Don't be so dramatic, Doña Clara. The others know the script by heart. They'll pull it off like a bunch of professionals. We're not lying about anything except the time it happened. He died around midnight, but for administrative reasons we made him die eight hours later."

The train was now descending through deep, sandy ravines. There were many curves and a few tunnels.

"What should we do about the guy in cabin one?" asked the steward upon entering Doña Clara's cabin.

"Is somebody there?" asked Doña Clara, surprised.

"An invalid, Doña Clarita," said the steward.

"Let him sleep in peace. He'll know soon enough."

Father Moreno changed his outfit. It was a stunning transformation: from Franciscan friar to someone who looked like a shopkeeper from the northern barrios of La Paz. Doña Clara was taken aback, as she had planned to ask him to administer the last rites to Nazario and console her daughter.

"I'm very sorry. Yesterday, I was an undercover union organizer. Here in Chile, I already feel much better. I think Alderete recognized me. He threatened to report me."

"Well, you obviously don't have to worry anymore."

Everyone came together in Alderete's cabin and struck up an impromptu conversation about the dead man. One of the waiters brought coffee and bread rolls.

"Last night, during the card game, he looked fine," said the waiter. "Life is a crapshoot."

"He had a weak heart," explained the Marquis.

"Did you know him well?"

"I knew him from Valparaíso. He stayed at my house."

"I hear he had a large fortune," said the waiter.

"The fortune will go to his widow and he'll take a blue party suit with him to heaven."

"In the end we're all nothing," said the waiter. He poured the coffee, adopting a sad face to fit in with the mourners around him.

When Tréllez left the cabin with several others, he turned toward the Marquis. "Will you write your ex-wife about Alderete's passing?"

"I'll be inspired," said the Marquis. "I'll find the most beautiful lines to tell her how I've forgotten all about how she cheated on me, and I'll describe in delicious detail how we tricked him at cards and the way he caught his sweet little wife in dear Ricardo's arms. With your knack for poetry, Tréllez, my friend, you can contribute a few satirical words to complete the letter."

"My pleasure."

"Let's go have breakfast," suggested Durbin.

"The women will take care of dressing him," said Ruiz.

At around 10 in the morning, the passengers pressed their faces against the windows and scanned the horizon. The blue of the sea was still far away, behind the gray hills. The sky was a dull blue and the hot air provided a prelude to the desert ahead of them. The train braked frequently as it negotiated the dips in the mountains. For the Bolivian passengers who had never seen the ocean before, this was one of the most breathtaking experiences of their lives. The train stopped in front of a small wood house surrounded by a couple of corrals in which a few donkeys milled around.

"An unexpected ending," said Durbin.

They were eating breakfast in the dining car. The atmosphere was pleasant.

"Don't tell me you feel bad," said Ruiz.

"I'd be a damn hypocrite if I did. But nor am I happy. A man's death is a serious matter."

"Things worked out for the Carletti girl," said Tréllez with a grin.

"I don't think she could have pushed Ricardo to this extreme," speculated Ruiz.

"The girl isn't stupid, but I don't think she's Machiavellian enough to spring that orgiastic scene on Nazario and expect it to have such a brutal effect on his blood pressure," said Tréllez.

Durbin began packing a pipe. He smiled maliciously. "Women's attitudes are and always will be a mystery to us. The Carletti girl might be an angel who just graduated from high school, but I wouldn't put my hands to the fire just because she told me to. The one who really fell for it like a sucker was young Ricardo. He became an actor in the tragedy without thinking, guided only by his libido."

"Here he comes," said Ruiz.

"You can see that Alderete's death has disturbed him. He thinks he's partially responsible," said Durbin. "If he'd only known that Alderete snake a little better . . ."

"It's not like you had to look at the man's résumé; one day with him was enough to know how low he was capable of going," said Tréllez.

"Good morning," greeted Ricardo.

"How are we feeling?" asked Durbin.

"I didn't sleep much," answered Ricardo. "I went by Alderete's cabin and saw his wife."

"Lourdes hardly came out yesterday," said Tréllez.

"The sight of Nazario made her uncomfortable. She had an almost uncontrollable urge to spit in his face," Durbin remarked.

"She'll be delighted," said Ruiz. "Ricardo, do you know the whole story about Durbin and Nazario?"

"I'll tell it to him in Arica," said the Irishman. "We shouldn't make him more upset."

"I actually don't feel very upset," said Ricardo.

"Have nothing do with it," commented Petko. "He catch wife in bed and that very common."

"You're telling me," said the Marquis.

"You catch your wife in act, but your heart not stop. It is matter of luck."

"Maybe if I'd surprised her at 16,000 feet, it would have turned out differently," said the Marquis. "At a lower altitude, everything seems less dramatic."

"When I saw you on train, I think you good kid," said Petko to Ricardo.

"He is a good kid," said Tréllez. "He's my nephew. Just because he bonked Gulietta doesn't make him an ogre."

"Please," said Durbin. "Don't talk like that. Bonked? What kind of a verb is that?"

"They say that a lot in Spain, my dear friend."

Still somewhat shaken by the previous night's catastrophe, Ricardo nonetheless had an impressive appetite. At his side, Tréllez curled his mustache upwards, which made him look like an idle Frenchman.

"There's nothing like the coast," he said. "It opens up my heart."

"I hope it open up your pocket too," said Petko. "That way you invite us to *pisco* sours at Hotel Pacífico."

"If you invite us, I'll introduce you to a girlfriend of mine who can make you happy," said Ruiz.

"My wife is waiting for me," said Tréllez.

"I'm talking about happiness, not tedium," Ruiz scoffed.

Dressed in their best outfits, the four women arrived in the dining car. Lourdes, whom Ricardo had seen a few times in the corridor looking melancholy and subdued, was now flashing her very best smile. A huge weight had been lifted from her shoulders; her sister had been avenged.

The women all sat down together. Doña Clara shot a distracted glance toward the gentlemen's table, tilted her head to one side, and then gazed at the arid hills.

At that moment, Rocha's half-leg appeared out of nowhere. His presence was a surprise to all; apparently, nobody had seen him before. But the steward affirmed that he had slept in cabin number one.

"His name is Rocha," added the steward.

"Strange guy," whispered Petko.

"He's just a cripple," said Ruiz.

"I see many in Soviet Union," said Petko. "Consequences of civil war."

Rocha settled in at a table by himself. His pinched expression seemed to indicate that he didn't want company.

"I'm sure we never saw that guy," commented Ruiz. "At least your wife came out from time to time."

"I don't like his face," said Durbin.

"Face of bastard," said Petko. "What he doing on train?"

* * *

The mountains finally gave way to tiny hills, and soon thereafter the ocean appeared.

"*Thalassa*! *Thalassa*! The sea!" exclaimed Tréllez.

It began as a thin blue line behind a strip of desert; as the train continued its descent, the blue gradually extended to infinity. Upon entering the Azapa Valley, a large expanse of vegetable farms came into clear view. The smell of the ocean filled the air and the passengers began preparing for arrival. Here and there, peasant laborers could be seen hard at work in the fields. Most of them were indigenous, probably Bolivian farmers who had immigrated in search of higher wages.

The train proceeded through an area of flatlands, which were bordered by small sandy hills scorched by the sun. A tramp steamer had just left port for the vast open sea.

"It was a fruitful trip," said Lourdes. "That Ricardo boy seems very excited about Gulietta."

"Let's hope he doesn't turn paranoid again," said Doña Clara.

"He'll get over it," Anita chimed in, "what with all the nice girls out there."

"I was special," said Gulietta.

"You combined passion and death," said Lourdes.

"Let's change the subject," suggested Doña Clara. "I think it would be best for me to arrange Nazario's burial, and you, Gulietta, should continue on your way. I hope the boat trip changes these ideas of yours."

"What ideas?"

"Don't even think about staying in Arica with dear Ricardo. You can't become a widow and marry again just like that . . ."

"Get married? To Ricardo? He's just . . . a friend."

"Some friend," said Anita.

"He was the dagger," said Lourdes. "The dagger that was needed to send that dog to hell."

The women all looked at Lourdes in silence. Her eyes were red with anger; when she lit a cigarette, they noticed her fingers were shaking.

"Take it easy, Doña Lourdes," soothed Anita. "It's all over now."

"What the women do with their boat tickets?" Petko asked Ricardo.

"Why don't you buy them at half-price?" said Ruiz.

"More oxygen for brain on coast, but not for Ruiz," said Petko.

"They tell me New Orleans is a beautiful city," said Tréllez.

"Don't torment the boy," interjected Durbin.

"Are you going to miss her?" asked Ruiz.

"Of course," said Ricardo.

"Ruiz has a hard time holding a conversation because of all that bad air he breathes in his poker games. If you knew his usual playing partners, you'd realize what I'm talking about," said the Marquis.

"You shouldn't take it so hard," said Tréllez, giving Ricardo several comforting pats on the back. "There will always be more girls and more trains."

They met in the corridor. Gulietta peered at him, hoping he would say something.

"You're already free," said Ricardo.

"It feels like he'll be following every one of my movements as long as he's above ground."

"Everything's simpler now," said Ricardo. "Imagine what you would've had to go through on the ship with Alderete on your back."

"I don't even want to think about it."

"You won't take that boat, will you?"

"I don't know. It depends on my mother."

"We'll see each other at the Hotel Pacífico . . . ?"

"Of course, my late husband booked a room for the night."

The whistle announced the proximity of the Port of Arica. The view was familiar to Ricardo; he had known it ever since he was a young boy. With the passing years, the city didn't seem to have changed much.

It was still a port without a dock. The cargo and passenger ships dropped anchor two hundred yards away from a mooring that the authorities had built with limited resources, but with a praiseworthy tenacity. Large barges transported cargo between ship and shore in a monotonous back-and-forth. From his cabin, Ricardo could see El Morro, a lookout rock that had become a symbol of the city. It was a serene town, one in which the calm was broken only by the rumblings of the sea.

The train skirted the edges of abandoned beaches. Near the shore, the waves played with greenish algae, which was devoured over and over again by the swirling tide. The dining car closed and the sleeping car passengers were chatting just outside the cabin where Alderete lay lifeless.

Rocha, elated by the proximity of the ocean, which he had never seen before, hopped from one side of his cabin to the other like a caged animal.

The train slowed its pace and eased into the station, which was awash with the summer sun. It stopped at the station's only platform. Ricardo's father, Don Enrique, accompanied by a good friend of his, Herr Koch, was waiting for Ricardo in front of the station and raised his arm when he saw his son. Koch was smoking a cigar and leaning on an ornate walking stick. There weren't many other people on the platform: a couple of families from the city waiting for half-breed women they had hired as maids; four ladies headed to the Marquis's nightclub, an upbeat and rambunctious bunch; and three policemen accompanied by a physician who would probably verify the death of Alderete. It wasn't every day that a corpse arrived on the La Paz–Arica train.

"How was the trip?" asked Ricardo's father.

"Different. A rich mine owner named Alderete died last night. His blood pressure went way up and it caused him to have a heart attack. I think these policemen are about to board the train."

"I knew that man by face," said his father.

"He was married to Gulietta Carletti, a girl my age."

"Ah! She probably had a lot to do with it," said Koch, laughing.

A luggage boy was waiting for them with a cart. He loaded Ricardo's suitcase and proceeded across the plaza toward the hotel, which stood on the other side, next to El Morro. A small train was returning from its endless labor of hauling enormous stone blocks for the dock which the authorities were building, gradually displacing the sea. The train whistled and passed through the station heading toward the opposite side of town. Ricardo breathed the damp ocean air. He recognized the navy building with a Chilean flag hanging from its watchtower. More luggage boys were waiting in front of the hotel.

"I said hello to your Uncle Tréllez and Durbin," said Ricardo's father. "Your mother couldn't come to the station because she went to the beach with your aunt. They don't want to miss out on a single day together at the ocean."

Hundreds of sea gulls were flapping around El Morro. Their incessant cawing triggered Ricardo's memories of previous summers. Seated on the crags of the gigantic rock, vultures watched the sea, poised to take a dive in pursuit of a fish or another tasty snack. On La Rambla, a couple of sailors in blue uniforms were out for a leisurely stroll.

"A boy named Canepa came here twice looking for you," said Don Enrique.

They entered the elegant lobby. The floor was marble and an impeccable carpet cut through the center of the hall and ascended an alabaster staircase; antique furniture adorned the enormous salon. Ricardo showed his passport to the concierge. The man greeted him and remarked that he had grown a lot in the past year. The bellboy accompanied Ricardo to the elevator while his father went for a drink in the little bar on the first floor, which served delicious ham-and-cheese sandwiches.

His father had booked a suite with an ocean view. It was filled with the morning sun and the warm ocean breeze. Ricardo walked to one of the windows and saw a fishing boat delving into the high seas, leaving in its wake tiny clouds of black smoke. One of the windows in his room had a magnificent view of the station, where Ricardo was able to make out Doña Clara, accompanied by the Marquis, entering an old taxi. Gulietta was seated on a kind of rickshaw being drawn by a little man.

It was headed across the plaza, toward the hotel. Ricardo went down to the lobby and waited for her.

Gulietta was in a daze: Accompanied by Ricardo, she walked around the lobby, the section reserved for card games, the smoking room, and even visited the kitchen. She looked out at the small adjacent park, where the city had set up swings for young children. She was amazed by how El Morro appeared to penetrate the ocean, and by the sight of so many vultures flying around its peak, which looked like it had been cut by a gigantic chisel. Ricardo walked her to the suite which had been reserved by Alderete. It was on the sixth floor, just like his.

"I'd like to take a bath before lunch," said Gulietta.

"Can I watch?"

"Of course not."

"I just want to see you naked in the bathtub."

Gulietta entered the bathroom and turned on the tub faucet. As there was no hot water except in the early morning, the water was cold. The bathtub was English, and it was made of caste iron with a ceramic finish. She took off her clothes and, once the tub had plenty of water, stepped in, letting out a soft squeal.

"You can come in," she called out.

Ricardo stared at her without saying anything. She closed her eyes and threw her head back. The water distorted the young curves of Gulietta's body. In the light of day, her sensuality was that of an innocent adolescent; there were no shadows—the luminosity conferred upon her an irresistible appeal.

"I don't want you to leave," said Ricardo.

"I'll be back in a couple of months. We'll see each other in La Paz. What's the problem?"

"That's a long time . . ."

She laughed.

"Where did your mother go?"

"She went to ask the authorities if she could bury Nazario here."

"How's the water?"

"Cold."

Ricardo kissed her forehead. "I think I'm in love with you. It's stupid but that's how it is."

"Then you'll have the patience to wait for me."

"I want to make love to you."

"Are you crazy? My mother could be back at any moment."

"Chilean bureaucracy might be less complicated than ours, but I don't think they'll wrap up the Alderete matter in the blink of an eye."

"Wait for me in the bedroom," said Gulietta.

Ricardo was starting to feel the need to have sex with only one girl. This had never happened to him before. He had never felt that imperious urgency, and it was unsettling. Alderete had caught the Gulietta syndrome, and now he had passed it on to Ricardo. Which of them truly had the last word?

She came out of the bathroom wearing a silk robe and lay down on the bed. Ricardo curled up at her side. She covered her breasts with her hands and tilted her face toward him. For the second time, she would experience that world of acute sensations, passionate words, animal cries, and rhythmic breathing.

Their bodies already knew each other, so everything was easier. Once the liaison was over, Ricardo said: "I can't get over the idea that you're boarding that ship."

"It's my mother's decision."

"Tell her that you want to stay in Arica for a while. You need to recover."

"From what?"

"Your husband just died."

"She knows I couldn't care less."

"What about the others?"

"Ricardo, you're the only important one."

"Think about me, then."

She got up and went back into the bathroom. "I'll see you at lunch," she called back.

Ricardo went downstairs and strolled down La Rambla. The pelicans were gliding behind the Naval Academy. He found himself next to the port where the fishing barges were anchored. At the edge of the wharf stood a tiny market in which squid, urchin, oysters, shellfish, and other seafood was sold. A pair of women were hawking fresh fish. Ricardo made the most of his time and drank a beer at the bar, which had a terrace that faced the unloading dock. The seamen were working at full throttle to prepare the barges to set sail on the rough waters.

"Hey there!"

It was Canepa, his buddy from Arica with whom he had spent many summers hanging out on the beaches and streets.

"I looked for you at the hotel," he said. "I saw your father."

"He told me. I just got in."

"I've been here for a week. I'm going to have to repeat the school year—I didn't behave myself." Canepa spent winters at an austere Jesuit boarding school in Santiago. In the summers he returned to Arica, where his father owned a grocery store. He was a loner, what psychologists call a "problem child." He wasn't a bad kid, but his behavior didn't always make sense. The two boys got along well because Ricardo didn't touch the sensitive spots of Canepa's somewhat troubled psyche. Canepa's two obsessions were the Colo Colo soccer team and betting. He bet on everything: horse races, chess, cock fights, and even trivial things, like who could make it to the street corner first or who could piss the farthest.

"Hey, man, I'm going out with a girl from Tacna who lives in Chinchorros. She has a sister."

"Give me a chance to breathe," said Ricardo. "Let's talk about it tomorrow."

Canepa was somewhat lanky, with permanently disheveled blond hair. His favorite outfit was a pair of worn-looking blue pants and a simple white shirt. He walked with a lazy gait and expressed himself using simple language colored by the word *dude*, which he used indiscriminately, even when talking with girls or older people.

"I'm the only guy left from our group in Arica . . . Hey, you look a little out of it," said Canepa.

"I met a girl on the train. She got my head spinning."

"Is she traveling alone?"

"No, with her mother. The old lady will decide whether or not she ships out tonight on one of the *Santas.*" There was no point in explaining what had happened on the train.

"Well, if she goes, there's always Gachi's sister. She doesn't travel anywhere; she doesn't even own a cent, dude."

"It's time for lunch," said Ricardo, ignoring his friend's suggestion. "I'll see you tonight on La Rambla."

"I thought we could go to the beach this afternoon."

"I'm dead tired."

"Okay, get some sleep. That way you'll be in shape for tonight."

They were waiting for him in the lobby: Ricardo's father, Uncle Tréllez and his wife Graciela, Durbin, and Lourdes. Also there was his mother, whom he hugged and kissed on the forehead. Fragile in appearance, she was nonetheless in excellent health and always on the move. The coastal climate did her good, as her usual paleness always gave way to a healthy tan. Aunt Graciela, who spent her time reading romance novels under the shade of an umbrella, maintained her parchment-colored skin. She was heavyset and wore abominable, out-of-style clothing, contrasting sharply with Tréllez's slight build and sophisticated fashion sense.

They headed up to the dining room. Nearly all of the tables were occupied. Upon seeing Doña Clara and Gulietta, Ricardo's father invited them to come sit with them. The waiters joined the two tables. The maître d'hôtel, a little man who smelled of talcum powder and had perfectly combed hair, handed them menus and then withdrew.

It was high season and the hotel mainly received businessmen from the south of the country, Peruvian and Bolivian tourists, government workers from Santiago, and the occasional military man with wife and children. An eccentric troupe of English travelers had settled into a nearby table; presumably, they would be catching one of the ships bound for Europe. At the head of the room was the orchestra, which consisted of a pianist with an ample mop of white hair, a violinist with a thin face, and a bored-looking accordionist.

They all opted for shrimp appetizers and Uncle Tréllez treated everyone to white German wine. Doña Clara had no choice but to relate, as straightforwardly as possible, the unexpected circumstances surrounding Alderete's death, omitting the erotic encounters between her daughter and Ricardo.

"His wake is today and tomorrow we bury him," she explained.

The band started up with a Viennese waltz and the conversation flowed pleasantly. Out of politeness, no one alluded to Gulietta's misfortune at having lost her husband. Everyone at the table knew that the girl had been sold off like a slave, then rescued by destiny, and that she was probably happy and dreaming about her freedom.

Gulietta sat down at Ricardo's side, took one of his hands in hers, and ran it over her thighs. He caressed the top of her skirt, before slipping his fingers underneath and brushing her pubis. She closed her eyes for a moment and then, with a look, ordered him to stop.

Gulietta enjoyed these interactions because they embarrassed Ricardo and kept his libidinous expectations alive. She derived a certain gratification from winding him up and leaving him hanging.

All one had to do was look at the boy to see he was in love. His eyes seemed to float in a cloud of juvenile passion. Meanwhile, in a single night, Gulietta had made the jump from adolescence to maturity, as if she had been touched by a magic wand. Her mother had ordered her to board the *Santa* that night: She had the ticket, the money, and an aunt waiting for her in New Orleans. She would stay a few months in the United States and return once every last bit of gossip around the life, passion, and death of Alderete had blown over. The only problem was Ricardo.

"I want to talk to you in the pool hall," she said to him.

Before leaving, they each enjoyed a dish of ice cream doused in chocolate sauce with a cherry on top. They drank fruit juice as well and had to put up with Durbin's tedious song and dance about the eventual reunification of Ireland. Under Doña Clara's uneasy gaze, Gulietta and Ricardo finally excused themselves from the table. Gulietta worried that if Ricardo became upset, his whole family would hear about the previous night's peccadilloes on the train, and, of course, so would all of La Paz, converting her into an outcast from Bolivian high society.

The pool hall was deserted at that hour. They settled into a beautiful couch facing the chimney, which was purely decorative, given that it never got cold in Arica.

"My mother decided that I should ship out," said Gulietta, holding her breath. "I'll be back in a few months."

"And what do you think?"

"I have to obey her."

"You're an adult."

"I'm not even twenty-one yet."

"That's nonsense. You're already a widow. What do *you* want?"

"To travel, forget about Alderete, and come back and find you again."

"Well . . . at least that makes your goodbye sweeter."

"Seriously, Ricardo, don't get sad, don't be difficult."

"I'm not getting sad or being difficult. It just seems rushed to me. You can take the next ship. The *Santas* anchor every week in Arica."

"The ticket is for today."

"Change it."

"It's not that simple."

"And your mother?"

"After burying him, she'll return to La Paz to take care of my affairs."

"A rich widow—what a delicious catch."

"You've acted like a gentleman up until now; don't ruin it. You have all my love."

Ricardo felt like his heart was tap dancing. "For how long?"

"Don't be a pain."

"Can I go to the ship to say goodbye?"

"It's just a freighter with a few cabins. It's not the *Queen of the Pacific*."

"I've never been on a ship before," said Ricardo.

"I just remembered that they don't give out visitor passes for the *Santas*."

"Are you sure?"

"Why would I lie to you?"

"All right," said Ricardo. "Sometimes I'm a little too forward."

She kissed him on the lips, caressed his hair, and looked at him tenderly. "I'm going to the wake with my mother."

"What time will you leave the hotel?"

"At around 7. The ship leaves at 8. I barely have time to buy stuff—you know, something to wear on board."

"I'll take a siesta," said Ricardo.

"I don't feel like going to the wake." Gulietta made a face like a spoiled rich girl, then turned to leave and said, "I'll see you later."

Ricardo went up to the window that looked out over the sea. The warm air carried the aroma of the waves crashing around El Morro. The *Santa Rita* suddenly appeared. He hadn't seen it before because it had been hidden behind that historic rock, the pride of this serene and quiet port.

It was a cargo ship like many others: ten thousand tons, the hull painted black, the deck a sparkling white, and a green smokestack. On the bow and the stern rose enormous cranes like giants with metal stingers. Several barges headed toward it. Motionless, Ricardo observed the freighter, which stopped some two hundred yards offshore, swaying side to side with a certain elegance.

The fading sun ducked behind the horizon. The sea, which had been a deep blue in the early afternoon hours, now acquired silvery tones. With the rising tide, the constant crashing of the waves could be heard off in the distance. Ricardo entered the small bar on the first floor. Tréllez and Durbin were there drinking cognac.

"Did you go to the wake?" asked Durbin.

"I don't know where it is . . ."

"At the end of 25 de Mayo. On the second floor of a wooden house. You'll see a hardware store on the ground floor."

"Why bother?" asked Tréllez.

"My wife is there and so is Anita," said Durbin. "The Marquis took care of everything."

"Doña Clara will probably slip him a few pesos," said Tréllez.

Petko came through the swinging door at that moment and sat down at the table.

"Where did you eat lunch?" asked Durbin.

"Customs official invite me to seafood restaurant." Petko lit a cigar and his beady eyes studied Ricardo. "Carletti girl already leave."

"I'm waiting for her," said Ricardo.

"She leave. I see her go."

"Impossible. She told me to wait for her."

"Yes! I accompany Doña Clara and Gulietta to barge that go to ship. Marquis too."

Ricardo stood up. He walked over to the concierge and asked for Gulietta. The man raised his eyebrows in a feminine gesture.

"She left for the ship half an hour ago."

"Are you sure?"

"Are you Señor Ricardo?"

"Ricardo Beintigoitia."

The concierge handed him a sealed envelope with his name on it. It was a short and cold missive from Gulietta affirming that she went looking for him everywhere, couldn't find him, and had no choice but to board her ship. She added that her mother was accompanying her, that she would probably return immediately to the wake, and that Gulietta would write to him from New Orleans.

"There's no way to visit the *Santa Rita?*"

The concierge was an annoying fellow. Not only did he maintain an obnoxious silence; he gave himself the luxury of looking at Ricardo somewhat flirtatiously. "Maybe," he said.

"How's that?"

"I can get an invitation for you."

"How much does it cost?"

"Nothing; it's a courtesy of the hotel."

The large barges swayed alongside the stern. Stevedores tossed thick ropes to the sailors of the *Santa Rita,* who proceeded to tie them to sturdy hooks on a wide opening on the hull. The boat in which Ricardo rode sidled up to the ship. After a series of maneuvers, one of the sailors seized a rope that the boatman had thrown him and tied the little vessel to the ladder. Ricardo climbed up to the deck. Once on board, he breathed in the ocean breeze, which smelled of the high seas. Three levels of solid iron stood before him, topped by the green smokestack that was still exhaling after the long journey from Valparaíso. Ricardo headed up to the second floor. A few vendor stands, somewhat upscale in appearance, formed a fan around the fountain, which was covered with climbing ivy. He walked up to a desk and asked a smiling, freckle-faced orderly for Gulietta's cabin.

"Upper deck," the guy answered.

Ricardo, for better or worse, found the way to the cabin through a jumble of corridors. He knocked and Doña Clara appeared.

"Hello, Ricardo, are you here with your family?"

"I'm alone."

"Come in. This is Gulietta's cabin. If I were traveling with her, I would be sleeping in the cabin right in front. I came to say goodbye to my daughter."

The room was spacious and comfortable. Along one side was a double bed, a closet in which Doña Clara had hung Gulietta's clothing, a Venetian-imitation oval mirror, and a desk.

"And Gulietta?"

"Out and about somewhere."

"Have you taken a look around?"

"To be honest, I'm very tired. Gulietta can tell me how beautiful the ship is in her next letter." She peered at herself in the mirror for a moment and applied some cream around her eyes.

Ricardo thought that Doña Clara wouldn't stay a widow much longer. He pictured her on the edge of a cliff and diving in headfirst. She looked good for her age, and with Alderete's money there would be no shortage of suitors out for a good time and a free ride. At forty years of age, a woman of her social standing, distinguished and well-preserved, was a prize that wouldn't pass unnoticed.

"I'm going to look for Gulietta to say goodbye," said Ricardo.

"Are you all right?"

"Yes, Doña Clara."

"It'll only be three months; then you'll see her again in La Paz."

Ricardo went down to the deck. He searched for her from bow to stern. At the rear of the *Santa,* there was a tiny pool and an American-style lounge. Gulietta was alone and drinking orange soda at the bar.

Ricardo stood quietly near the entrance. Meanwhile, one of the ship's officers appeared and sat down next to her. He ordered a beer and joked with the bartender, a scrawny black man. Gulietta glanced at the officer out of the corner of her eye and he returned the look. The man clearly had an effect on her. She became tongue-tied and her body trembled slightly. The officer appeared to be in his thirties and he had unusual features, if you assumed he was an American WASP. He had the look of an Italian who had grown eight inches taller than the average height in the motherland. He was handsome; and in his officer's uniform, he was doubly dangerous.

Ricardo, an intuitive young man, realized that Gulietta was in mortal peril, and that she would face it with great pleasure. The officer seemed to caress her with his eyes. There was a certain stiffness to his slender frame, though his movements were graceful and not without their charm. Gulietta stared at him, now seemingly hypnotized. Her eyes were only for him. People say that love and affection have nothing to do with the heart, which is only a muscle, but Ricardo's heart was in pain; he felt like an invisible hand was crushing it. He remained motionless, his eyes fixed on her. He had never seen her like this before, even in the moments he made love to her. She didn't look like the Gulietta he knew. The officer was drawing her into a space, the likes of which Ricardo had been unable to create. When she had been with him, she was always her own boss; she never lost control of her feelings. Dumbstruck, Gulietta listened devotedly to the officer's words, which he wove with the efficiency of a spider. There would be no point in approaching her.

Ricardo turned around, and as he was leaving, he heard her call his name.

Gulietta raised her hand, but Ricardo continued right on down the corridor toward the exit. Gulietta hurried from the bar and caught up with him.

"What's the matter?" asked Gulietta.

"Nothing. You're the one with the problem."

"I was just talking."

"Why did you tell me there was no way to come and visit the ship?"

Gulietta was hit by a torrent of vibrations emanating from Ricardo. His gaze was so penetrating that it made her face turn a deep red. She knew she had done the right thing in deciding to travel, whatever the cost. Ricardo's passion was thrilling, but also oppressive. If they stayed together, she feared there might be mutual suffering: He would compulsively try to force her to fit into his mold, while she would never abandon her newfound quest for freedom.

"Didn't you want to see me?" asked Ricardo.

"I was going to write as soon as I arrived in New Orleans."

"Don't make me laugh. You used me, Gulietta, as if I were a fool."

"You're so . . . intense . . ."

"Go back to your officer and stop lying. You already got what you wanted."

"I don't understand you."

Ricardo opened a hatch door that faced starboard and quickly descended the stairs to the rented craft that was waiting for him. The sun was slowly setting, fading like a doomed, sacred fire.

Ricardo kept an eye on the *Santa Rita* from his room. He was trying to defuse the violent emotions that were tormenting him and adopt an attitude of indifference in the face of the ship's imminent departure. But as the moment drew closer, this seemed impossible. For the first time in his life, he felt defenseless against a situation that was beyond repair. With a telescope, he would surely have seen her on deck, gazing at the city lights in the company of that officer. An irresistible, seafaring personage in the Anglo-Saxon tradition, he could have been a creation of Melville. Ricardo heard the ship's siren in the distance and managed to glimpse the anchor being raised over the bow. A large tugboat helped the *Santa Rita* turn around and head for the open sea. As the second siren sounded, Ricardo recalled the whistle of the Andean Express. The tugboat managed to point the ship's bow toward the horizon, beyond which the sun was almost gone. A final, definitive horn blast broke the small-town silence. Ricardo watched as the boat headed out into the ocean, leaving behind a trail of foam. Sea gulls circled overhead. He stood there silently until the boat's silhouette became one with the shadows. A fleeting period in his life, which had begun in La Paz the day before, had come to an end. The image of Gulietta at Central Station was vivid in his mind. He remembered the first time they exchanged glances there, the conversation in the dining car, the first caress, and that night when he first made love to her, accompanied by a pang of guilt. He imagined Gulietta's eyes, frozen in surprise, sweet-looking in orgasm. He was afraid he would never forget her, and that she would appear endlessly in his dreams. He didn't know her well, but their time together had been divine. Gulietta might go on to have a very beautiful life, but she would always find herself on a knife's edge. There would be a surprise around every corner, jealousy in every glance. It was too risky to live in a state of constant uncertainty. Loneliness would be hard to bear for a long while, but it was better to suffer now and forget . . . *If* he was able to forget.

The following day, a Friday, Doña Clara buried Alderete in the cemetery of Arica. Other than the Marquis and Anita, no one else witnessed Alderete's descent to his final resting place. It was a simple ceremony: Not a single tear was shed. Doña Clara had reserved her return ticket to La Paz for that day, and she would be joined by the Marquis, Anita, and the four hostesses who had come from Valparaíso. The Marquis put them up in a pension downtown, where they were preparing themselves for the daily grind that awaited them in the capital of the Altiplano.

The travelers who had occupied the sleeping car went their separate ways. Ruiz headed to Tacna to purchase merchandise, which he would later pass "under the table" through the border town of Desaguadero. The cash he had won in the poker game from Alderete wasn't too shabby, and he intended to double his small fortune by trading in contraband Peruvian cotton. Durbin and Lourdes flew in a DC-3 to Valdivia, where they planned to vacation for a while before embarking to Ireland. Rocha, the executioner, almost immediately caught a rickety bus bound for Iquique in search of the mulatta who would make him happy and use him as her one-legged pimp. With the sum he had received for eliminating the miner, he planned to open a tavern at which, obviously, he would be the number one consumer. He left Arica in a state of contentment, his conscience undisturbed.

Tréllez and Petko were still lodged at the Hotel Pacífico. After dispatching the freight that came from Germany to La Paz, Petko would dedicate himself to daily swims at La Licera, a popular beach, between the hours of 11 and 1.

It was a Saturday night. The film season had begun with a double-feature in the resort town's only movie theater. There were two American movies, a musical with Gene Kelly and a dark drama with Humphrey Bogart and Lauren Bacall.

When his family retired to the hotel, Ricardo decided to take a walk on La Rambla. As always, Canepa was there waiting for him. He introduced him to his girlfriend and her sister, a pale, quiet young woman named Soledad who glanced suggestively at Ricardo. They agreed to meet up the next afternoon at the sisters' beach house in Chorrillos.

The sisters excused themselves on the pretext of going home to listen to a radio soap opera. Ricardo and Canepa smoked and looked out at the ocean, which was barely illuminated by a timid summer moon. Ricardo wanted to be alone and said goodbye to Canepa, promising to join him on Sunday at the girls' house.

He headed for the bar on the ground floor of the Hotel Pacífico, which had two entrances: one from the street and the other from the hotel lobby. They were serving excellent coffee, which they imported from Colombia. A bald, chubby bartender was sweating behind the counter when Ricardo arrived. He was leafing through an Argentine sports magazine and glanced occasionally at the plaza, which was dimly lit by a pair of art noveau streetlamps.

"Last night there was a temblor," said the waiter. "Did you notice it?"

"No," said Ricardo.

"There's a temblor almost every day."

"I've been coming here since I was seven years old. Temblors don't surprise me."

"You've probably never been in an earthquake. As a child, I lived through Chillán. I was so scared my hair fell out."

At that moment, Petko had just stopped around the corner, next to some planters containing roses and carnations. He was smoking. He took a long look at El Morro and proceeded into the bar. He was dressed in a linen suit, which was both elegant and spotless. He took off his hat, and as he placed it on a chair, he said: "Mind if I sit down?"

"Of course not," replied Ricardo.

"Family asleep?"

"We went to the movies," said Ricardo.

"You very depressed. I not see why."

"I'm thinking about what happened on the train."

"And?"

"Maybe if he hadn't surprised us in bed, Alderete would still be alive."

"*Khuya!*" Petko exclaimed. He ordered a cognac and a small coffee and waited in silence for the chubby guy to serve him. Then: "I have something to say you if you allow me. I don't like to see you like that, seem like you will have same face at Club de La Paz café."

Ricardo nodded.

"Now they leave, it best to tell truth."

"Uncle Tréllez is still in Arica."

"He not part of this." Petko sipped the cognac and the coffee. "I feel good. Ocean whet appetite."

Ricardo became impatient. "What were you going to tell me?"

"You, Ricardo, had nothing to do with death. He not die of heart attack."

"Then what did he die of?"

Petko bit into his cigar with relish. "They kill him."

"*They* did?"

Petko's gray, squirrel-like eyes looked away. "It seem made up, but is true. They killed. I saw everything," he said, smiling.

"How? Who?"

"Swear you not repeat what I say now because it about honorable person."

"Honorable?"

"The one who killed was not very honorable, but the one with idea was . . ."

Ricardo ordered a cognac; he'd never had one before. The chubby waiter offered him a cigarette and asked if he wanted more coffee.

"Please," said Ricardo.

"When Alderete go to his cabin after we won poker, I have to go to bathroom at end of car," said Petko. "I got up and go to one at end of dining car. It was full. I wait, but really need to piss, so I go to bathroom in my sleeping car. Piss and leave, what did I see?"

"What did you see?"

"Cripple Rocha leave cabin. He look all around, but not notice I was there. Rocha go to cabin of Alderete, who just leave yours, after see erotic scene. He entered cabin. I go slowly toward door and hear short but fatal conversation."

"Rocha killed him?"

"Rocha killed in two or three minutes. Fast. He say few words to Alderete and send him to other world. I hide myself again in bathroom. Rocha leave happy and return to cabin. I stay silent."

"Unbelievable!" said Ricardo.

Petko blew a puff of cigar smoke into the air. "Cuban tobacco is best. Nothing compare."

Ricardo burned his throat with a sip of cognac. He was astonished, but he knew Petko wasn't lying. Why would he? He had no reason to.

"Then, before Gulietta go out into corridor, other person appear."

"Who?"

"Doña Clara."

"And what did she do?"

"She look around, enter Alderete cabin, leave, and slide envelope under Rocha door. Probably money."

Ricardo finished the cognac and asked for one more.

"Not drink cognac like that. You have to sip. It not like beer."'

"Incredible . . ."

"Why incredible? Alderete leave her husband penniless. Kill him too, but little by little. Better to die like Alderete, in single moment. Not have time even to think about all terrible things he did. Now feel better?"

"Yes, but I'm puzzled. Doña Clara, she's a classy woman . . ."

"That is it . . . for being classy woman, send Alderete to hell. Ricardo, promise you not say nothing. On your word—if not, Doña Clara in trouble, even though no proof. Alderete already underground. End of story."

"Gulietta . . . did she know?"

"I do not think so. She sexy girl, but not diabolical. You the same."

"Thanks for telling me. I'll sleep better now."

"Even though you think a lot about Carletti girl."

"It'll pass with time."

"There are a lot of girls, you very young. Not run out of chances."

"You didn't tell anyone else?"

"I am discreet guy."

Petko called the bartender, who was preparing to close down. A peaceful time of night, with the sea breeze alleviating the heat.

"It on me," said Petko.

"Will you stay a few more days?"

"Go back Tuesday on train. I finish everything I have to do."

And so began Ricardo's vacation: mornings at the beach, siestas in the afternoon, social outings with Canepa, evenings in the company of his parents and the Tréllez's. There were the visits to the port, the daily double-features at the movie theater, and the sleepless nights thinking about Gulietta. With every passing day, though, the memories receded, little by little, until only faint images remained . . .

I wish to thank my father, John Althoff, who introduced me to Bolivia and whose love and support made it possible for me to pursue this adventure.
—A.A. (translator)

Also available from Akashic Books

AMERICAN VISA
a novel by Juan de Recacoechea
260 pages, trade paperback original, $14.95

"Dark and quirky, a revealing excursion to a place over which 'the gringos' to the north always loom."
—*New York Times Book Review*

"Beautifully written, atmospheric, and stylish in the manner of Chandler . . . a smart, exotic crime fiction offering."
—George Pelecanos, author of The *Turnaround*

THE UNCOMFORTABLE DEAD
a novel by Subcomandante Marcos & Paco I. Taibo II
268 pages, trade paperback original, $15.95

"Great writers by definition are outriders, raiders of a sort, sweeping down from wilderness territories to disturb the peace, overrun the status quo and throw into question everything we know to be true . . . On its face, the novel is a murder mystery, and at the book's heart, always, is a deep love of Mexico and its people."
—*Los Angeles Times Book Review*

ADIOS MUCHACHOS
a novel by Daniel Chavarría
246 pages, trade paperback original, $13.95
*Winner of a 2001 Edgar Award

"A zesty Cuban paella of a novel that's impossible to put down . . . a great read."
—*Library Journal*

"A steamy, sexy, kinky, pulpy mix of comedy, mystery, and murder."
—*Booklist*

"Daniel Chavarría has long been recognized as one of Latin America's finest writers."
—Edgar Award–winning author William Heffernan

THE AGE OF DREAMING

a novel by Nina Revoyr

320 pages, trade paperback original, $15.95

"*The Age of Dreaming* elegantly entwines an ersatz version of film star Sessue Hayakawa's life with the unsolved murder of 1920s film director William Desmond Taylor. The result hums with the excitement of Hollywood's pioneer era . . . Reminiscent of Paul Auster's *The Book of Illusions* . . . [with] a surprising, genuinely moving conclusion."

—*San Francisco Chronicle*

SOUTH BY SOUTH BRONX

a novel by Abraham Rodriguez

292 pages, trade paperback original, $15.95

"A street poet like Bob Dylan, Rodriguez has woven a lyrically inventive and sophisticated noir . . . Full of unforgettable one liners, *South by South Bronx* manages to film a neighborhood filled with beauty, danger, and magic. One fearless, hell of a literary mystery novel."

—Ernesto Quiñonez, author of *Bodega Dreams*

HAVANA NOIR

edited by Achy Obejas

360 pages, trade paperback original, $15.95

Brand new stories by: Leonardo Padura, Pablo Medina, Carolina García-Aguilera, Ena Lucía Portela, Arnaldo Correa, Achy Obejas, Miguel Mejides, and others.

"A remarkable collection . . . Throughout these 18 stories, current and former residents of Havana deliver gritty tales of depravation, depravity, heroic perseverance, revolution, and longing in a city mythical and widely misunderstood."

—*Miami Herald*

These books are available at local bookstores.
They can also be purchased online through www.akashicbooks.com.
To order by mail send a check or money order to:

AKASHIC BOOKS

PO Box 1456, New York, NY 10009

www.akashicbooks.com, info@akashicbooks.com

(Prices include shipping. Outside the U.S., add $8 to each book ordered.)